Dear Reader,

I think we've all experie[nced] [a] [first] love sometime in our liv[es] [the] [boy] [we] were too scared to spe[ak] [to] [who] [made] your day just that little bit brighter. For my Kate that "boy" was Gideon Manser.

I hope you ache for her—for them both—because life has hit them hard. In reality things do not always work out the way we would wish, but in my story Gideon and Kate have the happy ending they richly deserve.

The Isle of Wight, where this book is set, is a real place. My husband worked on it for a couple of summers, and my family and I escape there whenever we can. If you stand at the bottom of England and look out to sea, you will see it. Just twenty-three miles by thirteen miles, it's a truly magical place. I can't think of many places more perfect to live out a "happy ever after."

Much love,

Natasha

Harlequin Romance® is thrilled to bring you another
sparkling new book from British author

Natasha Oakley

Her poignant and emotional writing will
tug on your heartstrings.

Books by Natasha Oakley

Don't miss any of our special offers. Write to us at the
following address for information on our newest releases.

Harlequin Reader Service
U.S.: 3010 Walden Ave., P.O. Box 1325, Buffalo, NY 14269
Canadian: P.O. Box 609, Fort Erie, Ont. L2A 5X3

A FAMILY TO
BELONG TO

Natasha Oakley

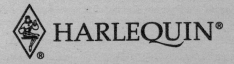

TORONTO • NEW YORK • LONDON
AMSTERDAM • PARIS • SYDNEY • HAMBURG
STOCKHOLM • ATHENS • TOKYO • MILAN • MADRID
PRAGUE • WARSAW • BUDAPEST • AUCKLAND

ISBN 0-373-03878-X

A FAMILY TO BELONG TO

First North American Publication 2006.

Copyright © 2005 by Natasha Oakley.

www.eHarlequin.com

Printed in U.S.A.

NATASHA OAKLEY told everyone at her primary school she wanted to be an author when she grew up. Her plan was to stay at home and have her mum bring her coffee at regular intervals—a drink she didn't like then. The coffee addiction became reality, and the love of storytelling stayed with her. A professional actress, Natasha began writing when her fifth child started to sleep through the night. Born in London, U.K., she now lives in Bedfordshire with her husband and young family. When not writing, or needed for "crowd control," she loves to escape to antique fairs and auctions. Find out more about Natasha and her books on her Web site www.natashaoakley.com

CHAPTER ONE

THE wind tasted salty on her lips and the ice-cold rain pitted her cheeks. Kate Simmonds stared out at the slate-grey sea and felt her hair flick painfully around her face.

She was coming home.

Too late.

Aunt Babs was dead.

She lifted one shaking hand to push back her hair. A week ago everything had been so different, or had seemed that way. Then there'd been time. She had known she'd make the trip back home some time— just not yet. She wasn't ready. Even now. And Aunt Babs had understood. She really had.

But now it was too late.

Kate leant against the metal bar of the upper ferry deck and looked out to sea. An immense grey vastness stretching out before her. It put everything into perspective somehow. Made all her bitter angst seem rather unimportant and petty. She *should* have made time.

Aunt Babs had given her a home. She'd taken an awkward, angry little ten-year-old into her house and loved her as though she'd been her own. A foster mum in a million. Kate knew she'd deserved more from her than the weekly phone call and the occasional trip to London. It was just one more regret to add to the pile she was accumulating in her life.

It must be almost six years since she'd made this

trip. She'd not meant to stay away so long. *Six years!*
So much had changed in that time. *She* had changed.
She was barely recognisable from that twenty-two-
year-old Katie. She'd passed through Katie, Kay and
Katherine before becoming Kate. Reinvented. Kate
Simmonds. Poised. Elegant. In control of her life.

If only that were true. Inside she still lived with the
same cankerous uncertainties and a desperate desire
to belong. Still carried the scars of rejection. And
now, of course, there was something more. Something
even deeper. A more recent pain that seared like a
branding iron. She pushed her hands deep in the pockets of her long black coat and turned away from the
overwhelming greyness of the March sky.

Just a handful of tourists had ventured outside to
eagerly watch the Isle of Wight appear in the distance.
They stood clustered together under a canopy of
clashing umbrellas. Dimly she was aware of a questioning glance directed at her, then a half-smile as
though the elderly lady in the red anorak thought she
might know her.

Kate looked away. She didn't. It was an illusion—
like so much of her life. She didn't want the inane
conversation she knew would follow. She wanted to
be left alone with her thoughts, however painful.

Abruptly Kate turned and walked back across the
deck, pulling open the heavy metal door. The high
heels on her suede boots made the steep steps down
difficult and her black coat spread out behind her like
a flowing cape.

Below, the passenger lounge smelt of chips and
stale cigarettes but it was good to be out of the bitter
wind. Kate shook out her hair and unwound her long

burnt-orange scarf before joining the crocodile of people waiting in line for something to drink.

'If you want coffee you're in the wrong queue.'

Her head whipped up at the sound of a male voice and she stared up into the face of Gideon...Manser.

His name fell effortlessly into place. She remembered him perfectly. His intense blue eyes and angular features. The small indentation in the centre of his chin. A man with more sex appeal than the average movie star. And the object of her unrequited teenage fantasies.

'The machine's broken down this side,' he said calmly, a faint smile pulling lines in his strong cheeks.

Gideon Manser.

Instinctively her hand went to her hair; she was uncomfortably aware it hung damp and limp about her face. She'd have known him anywhere. He hadn't altered at all. Or perhaps he had a little. He was slightly thinner. Tired-looking. Slightly worn at the edges. But he was still sexy. Very sexy indeed.

'Thank you,' she managed.

She could remember, all too clearly, what a complete and utter fool she'd made of herself when he'd first arrived on the island. At seventeen she'd thought he was the most gorgeous thing to have ever walked the planet—and she couldn't have made it much plainer.

He was older than her. Much older. A top London chef who'd lived in France and Italy. He'd had all the glamour and sophistication her young heart had craved. Just thinking about how she'd behaved made her long to curl up in a ball and howl with humiliation.

Strangely he didn't seem so old to her now. With

the magic of adulthood she seemed to have caught him up. Kate straightened her shoulders. 'It's Gideon, isn't it?' Kate hesitated. 'Gideon Manser? Do you remember me? I'm Kate. Kate Simmonds? Well, I was always called Katie. You perhaps don't remember me. I—'

Shut up. Just shut up. Stop babbling on, she thought desperately. It would be better if he didn't remember her.

She bit down on her lip. He probably wouldn't remember. Why should he? He hadn't been interested in her. They must have laughed at her—him and Laura. Or felt sorry for her—which would be worse.

'Of course I remember you,' he said, stretching out his hand.

Hell! She felt a flush mottle her neck as she stretched out her own hand.

'It would be difficult not to.' He smiled and his fingers wrapped around hers. 'Babs has...had,' he corrected swiftly, 'photographs of you everywhere and Debbie made sure everyone knew you were on the television now. Half the island is fascinated by your reports from the States each week. You're a celebrity. A local girl made good.'

Kate looked down at her boots. 'Oh, right.' She should have guessed she'd be a minor celebrity on the Isle of Wight. Debbie had just loved it when she'd landed the job as LA correspondent and started making weekly television reports. Couldn't hear enough of who was doing what and with whom.

And Aunt Babs had just been proud. The thought speared her with guilt. She should have come back to the island before now. It would have meant so much to the woman who'd changed her life so dramatically.

Gideon looked across at the other queue. 'We'd better get in line or there won't be time to have a coffee.'

'I suppose not.'

She felt her stomach twist in a nervous flutter. *Gideon Manser.* Why did he have this effect on her still? She was twenty-eight years old, for heaven's sake. Her world was peopled with sexy men. She'd interviewed most of them. He wasn't anything special.

And yet…

She fiddled with the strap of her handbag. It was probably the place. It brought back memories she hadn't thought of in years. Rocked her off balance. Or maybe Gideon was just a symbol of what she couldn't have. Something else she couldn't have, she amended silently.

She looked back at him. His jacket collar was pulled up against the cold, his jeans were dark and his hands were…well, they were beautiful.

He reached across for the tray. 'Debbie said you'd be coming home for the funeral.'

'Y-yes.'

'Was it difficult to get away?' Kate reached across for a tray of her own but he stopped her. 'Don't bother. I'll get these.'

'You don't have to. I—' She broke off and let her hand fall back. 'Thank you.'

'So—' he turned to smile at her '—was it difficult?'

His smile was like a gateway to a time tunnel. She felt as if she was shooting back through the years at the speed of light. So many memories flashing by. The kind that came up to bite you when you were least expecting it.

At seventeen she'd fantasized about what it would be like to kiss him. At night she'd closed her eyes and pretended he was her pillow and imagined his voice telling her how much he loved her. She pulled her gaze away from his lips, embarrassed.

She'd been an idiot. It wasn't surprising a man of twenty-six hadn't been interested in an adolescent seventeen.

'Did you find it difficult to get away for the funeral? Debbie thought you might be too busy. Not be able to make it.'

Kate stuffed her hands down into the depths of her coat pockets. 'Oh, no.'

'No?' he repeated.

He seemed to be watching her critically. Probably wondering why she couldn't have visited Aunt Babs and Debbie more often if it were so simple.

On the surface she'd just packed her bags and left without a backward glance. Only a few very special people knew why. And they wouldn't have told a soul.

'How long are you staying for?' he asked.

'Until Wednesday. Not long. I've got to get back to London...' The line moved forward and Kate reached for a china cup. It was good to have something sensible to do with her hands. She rested it on the metal grid and pushed the 'coffee white decaf' button.

'Not going back to the States immediately, then?'

'No.' She put the cup down on a saucer and made an effort to relax. 'And how are you?' She watched his strong hands go through the same procedure as she'd done.

'Good.' He hesitated. 'You heard about Laura, I suppose?'

Her stomach did a somersault as the floor appeared to disappear beneath her feet. *Damn it! She had heard.*

With crushing clarity she remembered Debbie's tearful phone call. The shock of hearing that Laura was dead. How could she have been so thoughtless? 'Yes, I—'

'She died.'

'Y-yes, I know. I'm so sorry.' She pulled her hand through her hair. 'I meant to write at the time but...' She trailed off weakly.

But...she'd been busy with her own trauma. Her own grief had been so intense when Richard left that she'd struggled to believe anyone could be hurting as much as she was. She'd had no compassion left for anyone but herself.

Not even Debbie, who'd been distraught at having lost her friend. With a pang she realised she'd scarcely given Gideon a thought.

She looked up at his face. His pain was there. Etched on his face. In his eyes. And there was nothing she could really say to help him. How did you even begin to say something sensible to a man who'd lost the wife he'd loved?

His smile was tight. Forced. 'Two years ago. Not long after Tilly was born.'

'I know. I'd just gone to LA. Debbie rang me...' Thankfully the queue moved on again. 'I'm sorry. I—'

'Do you want a muffin?' He cut her off. 'Or perhaps some chocolate? You're usually safer in these places if it's wrapped.'

Kate looked up. One moment death, the next muf-
fins. It was strange how people did that. Moved in
and out of grief. It was as though they couldn't bear
to think about it for too long. Just touched it and then
had to turn away before the pain became too great.

'Nothing. Thanks.'

He reached out for some biscuits. 'I missed breakfast. It was an early start,' he said by way of expla-
nation.

Kate nodded. The queue moved on again and they
reached the till point.

Laura Bannerman had had everything: two parents
who loved her, a beautiful home, her own pony,
blonde hair, no acne—and Gideon.

It was difficult to think of her as dead. Horrible
now to think how much she'd hated her. Well, envied
was a more accurate description. She hadn't *hated*
her. Her life had seemed enchanted, that was all, and
if she could have waved a magic wand and changed
places with Laura she would have.

But not now. Poor Laura was dead and Gideon a
widower. No one could have foreseen that coming.
She would have liked to ask what she'd died of but
knew she couldn't.

He picked up the tray. 'Do you mind where we
sit?'

'Not at all.'

'Smoking—'

'Non-smoking,' she cut in quickly. 'Gave up last
year. One year, nine months, fourteen days and count-
ing.'

'Congratulations.'

'Thank you.'

Did he remember about that? She'd started smoking that summer in a desperate, foolish attempt to look older. Who knew why she'd thought he'd be impressed? It hadn't worked but she'd started a difficult habit to break.

Gideon carried the tray across to a table by one of the windows. Two long bench seats were either side. 'Will this do?'

'It's fine.' Kate unbuttoned her coat and sat down. 'Are you staying with Debbie?'

'I don't know yet.'

'Ah.' He unwrapped his biscuit before snapping it in half. 'Are you sure you don't want some?'

'I don't eat biscuits.'

'Ever?'

'Empty calories,' she said, picking up her cup. 'It's all about discipline.'

Gideon frowned. *Discipline.* It didn't surprise him she should say something like that. Discipline was probably the mantra by which she lived her life.

Not many people managed the breakthrough into television from radio. It took determination and a single-minded, focused kind of commitment. The kind that made one careless about the feelings of others.

A shadow passed across his face. He knew all about that kind of ambition. The human cost of it…

What was the point of Kate Simmonds coming back to the island now? When Babs was dead? It was too late. She'd been too busy when it had mattered to visit the people who loved her.

Just as he'd been too busy to notice how ill Laura had become.

'No chocolate? That's quite a sacrifice,' he said, looking back at Kate. Had she really not noticed how much Babs and Debbie had wanted her to visit? It seemed unbelievable.

He studied her. She was going to make quite a stir on the island. Her clothes were expensive, her hair obviously cut by an expert, her make-up impeccable and her nails acrylic. Still had the same brown eyes though. The ones that looked out at everything and everyone with such pain and made you feel as if you were kicking a puppy.

'Hanging out with Hollywood's "beautiful people" is enough to give anyone neurosis about their weight.' Kate shrugged and sipped the bitter liquid before pulling a face at her coffee. 'That's disgusting! Like drinking tar.'

He smiled. 'It's the worst coffee on the planet. Had you forgotten? You've been away too long.'

Kate's face relaxed and her eyes lost some of their tension. She put the cup back down on the tray. 'Do you still own the Quay Inn?'

'Yes. We're in the Michelin Guide with one star. We've had that for a few years now and we're hoping for a second.'

Hoping. That was a lie if ever there was one. He was working every hour God sent to make it happen—and shunting his girls all over the place. Babs had told him it was 'short-term pain for long term gain' but was it really worth it? He rubbed a tired hand across the back of his neck.

'That's fantastic.'

'Yes.' He looked down at the table. It *was* fantastic. It was his lifetime ambition. *Their* ambition. His and Laura's. But without her it didn't seem worth having. 'Laura and I always hoped… It seemed important at the time. But…well…'

Kate looked away, suddenly feeling as if she was stepping on eggshells. She could feel his sadness radiating from him. How pointless it all was. She knew he would trade it all, all his success, if he could just have his wife back. She understood something of how that felt.

The silence stretched on. 'How old are your children now?' she asked in a rush. As soon as the words left her mouth she wished she could take them back. She knew, almost to the day, how old his eldest child was.

'Jemima is five.'

Laura had been pregnant on her last visit to the island. Glowing with excitement. It had hurt.

'And Matilda is three,' he said quietly. 'Just three.'

Kate watched him bow his head as though the weight of the world was resting on his shoulders. A strange phrase that. Whenever she heard it she wondered what it actually meant—but looking at Gideon she knew exactly.

And then he picked up his coffee and drank without flinching. For a man who could taste the most intricate food combination with complete precision that was quite a feat.

'They're pretty names.'

'Laura…' His voice broke. 'Laura picked them. I was going to choose the boys'. We'd hoped to have more children. Maybe another couple.' He shrugged and Kate could feel his desperation to return to normal. Heard the steadying breath he took. 'But it wasn't to be. You haven't got any? Children?' he clarified when she didn't immediately answer.

Kate almost flinched. It was a reasonable question.

In time, no doubt, she'd get used to people asking it. 'No. No children.'

She could have added she would never have children. Couldn't. But it was impossible to formulate those words. It was as though it would become more real if she said it out loud. Make it true. Which was illogical because you couldn't change a medical fact. She would *never* have children.

'No time, I suppose. With your career.'

She gave a swift smile. One she knew didn't reach her eyes. 'It certainly keeps me out of mischief.'

'A significant other?'

'Not so you'd notice,' she answered quickly with a furtive glance out of the window. *Not any more.*

This couldn't go on much longer. With every moment the island was drawing closer. It was too uncomfortable meeting Gideon again. 'Too busy working to have a relationship,' she lied.

Gideon sat back on the bench. 'You got your dream. It must be very exciting.'

Exciting? She wanted to laugh. You could describe it like that, she supposed, if you ignored all the endless waiting around to interview someone who didn't much want to be interviewed. The sickening feeling when they only answered you in monosyllables and you knew you had to make something interesting out of it. Of course there were moments. Exciting moments.

Kate let her forefinger play with the edge of her saucer. But they didn't fill the void she felt in her life. There was no way to explain how she felt about doing yet another interview with yet another 'star' promoting yet another film. In the greater scheme of things it just didn't matter. Somewhere along the line it had lost its glamour. And all the time she had a different dream. Another dream. One that could never come true.

'I've been very lucky,' she compromised.

Gideon's mouth twisted into the half-smile she remembered. Hell, it was sexy. The effect was like a light bulb going on.

'Luck takes work. No one knows that better than I do. The Quay Inn isn't a success by chance. I put in long hours to make it happen. Sacrificed a lot.'

'Sometimes I think there's an element of fate about it though. Just being in the right place at the right time. Most of my opportunities have come about by chance.' She looked out of the window again, glad to see how close they were to land. *Not much further and she could escape.*

'It helps if chance is on your side,' he replied, breaking off as a lady in a red anorak approached them, her eyes on Kate. 'Can I help?'

She waited until Kate looked up before saying hesitantly, 'I'm sorry to disturb you, but are you the lady from the television? The one who does the weather?'

The expression on Gideon's face almost made Kate laugh but she answered with a calm smile, grateful for the interruption. 'Entertainment news. That's my slot. Hollywood gossip.'

In the two weeks she'd been back in London she'd almost got used to this kind of thing happening. In LA she'd passed completely unobserved.

The woman turned round to nod triumphantly at her friend, who was hovering uncertainly by the evacuation notice. Then she turned back to rummage in her anorak pocket, pulling out a notebook and pen.

'Would you mind signing this? I said to Yvonne—

she's the lady in the brown coat—over there.' She
pointed. 'With the glasses. I said to Yvonne when we
were on the ferry deck that I recognised you. I always
watch your bit. We both do. She said she didn't think
it was you. But I'm very good with faces.'

Kate suppressed the bubble of laughter building inside her as she flicked over the shopping list on the
top page. 'Of course I'll sign it.' Out of the corner of
her eye she could see Gideon watching in apparent
disbelief. 'What's your name?'

'Cynthia.' Her chest puffed out in gratification as
she saw Kate begin to write her name. 'Cynthia
Puttock. Mrs Cynthia Puttock.'

Kate handed the notebook back with a wide smile.
'It's nice to meet you, Cynthia.'

Cynthia looked at the autograph with immense satisfaction. 'Would you mind…' she began as a new
thought occurred to her. 'Would you mind if I had
my picture taken with you? My husband isn't going
to believe I met you.'

She didn't wait for Kate to reply before she was
waving over her shoulder at her friend, ignoring the
tannoy which was asking for all drivers to return to
their cars.

'It won't take a moment. Yvonne, would you—?'
She broke off and turned impulsively towards Gideon.
'Would you take the picture? Yvonne, you stand
there.'

Kate decided to give in with good grace. She
flicked her hair back off her face and stood up, placing herself between the two women. It was as close
to being a celebrity as she was going to get. As close
as she wanted to get. It made her feel uncomfortable.

She watched as Gideon was given a rudimentary introduction to the stranger's camera.

'There,' he said, moments later. 'I hope I've got you a photo.'

'Thank you very much. I—'

The tannoy cut off their gratitude. 'We'd better go down to the cars,' Kate said apologetically. 'It's very nice to have met you both.'

Gideon's hand moved to fit into the small of her back and he guided her towards the yellow exit. 'Does that happen often?' he asked quietly.

'Only since I've been back in the UK.' Her face broke into a genuine smile as real laughter bubbled up. 'But don't worry, I'm not letting it go to my head. How can I? I'm on the page after carrots and potatoes and she thought I was the weather girl! Nice to know I'm memorable.'

He laughed and Kate turned to look at him. He looked much younger when he laughed. Handsome. She hadn't thought about him for years and yet, seeing him again, it was as though she were seventeen again. She was completely aware of his hand resting in the small of her back. He was hardly touching her and yet…

She moved away, her smile dying on her face. 'We'd better get back to the cars. It was nice to see you again.'

'And you.'

'After such a long time.' Kate reached into her bag for her car keys. 'Oh, and thank you for the coffee.'

'It was a pleasure,' he said, pulling open the door down to the car deck.

Kate held her long coat off the steps as she walked down in front of him. At the bottom she turned back to him. 'Well, goodbye. I'm glad we bumped into each other.'

'I wouldn't worry too much about goodbye,' he said, holding the door open for the couple behind. 'We're bound to meet again.'

'A-are we?' Kate asked, suddenly feeling foolish.

'Inevitably. Debbie's looking after my girls today.' He broke off as someone loudly tooted their car horn. 'We'd better hurry and get to our cars. People are getting irritated.'

Kate turned obediently and cut through towards her little green MG.

'Nice car,' she heard Gideon say, and felt vaguely pleased. Though why it should matter that he liked her car she didn't know. She forced herself not to look back at him but climbed elegantly into her low-slung car.

Meeting Gideon again had been a bizarre experience. Unexpected. Though there was no reason why he shouldn't be on the car ferry. Lots of locals popped back and forth to the mainland. It was just she'd been stealing herself for the funeral. She hadn't expected to meet anyone yet.

She waited while the heavy doors of the ferry opened, watching as the line next to her was sent out first. How could she have been so stupid not to remember about Laura the minute she'd recognised him?

She leant forward and rested her head on the steering wheel, closing her eyes in mortification. It seemed it was her destiny to act like an idiot when she was around him. Maybe some things never changed, however many years passed.

She started the engine and put it in gear. His face

had looked so bleak. But then what did she expect? His wife had died. It didn't get much worse than that.

Certainly she'd nothing to complain about in comparison. Not even Richard's leaving could really compare to Gideon's loss. Kate's hands gripped on the steering wheel as a wave of sadness washed over her. It was never far away. Always lapping at the edge of her consciousness. Making her feel dissatisfied—and angry.

At least Gideon had his children. She would never have that. Never have a family of her own. Never have anyone really love her...

Kate let her car roll forward as the van in front started to move off. And now she had to face Debbie.

There was the bump where the ramp joined land—and she was back on the island. Back where people would look at her and remember she'd been a foster girl. Unwanted. An object of pity. The one with head lice.

Or she had been until Aunt Babs had declared war on them. A bitter battle which had involved her spending hours with her head over the bath, a fine tooth comb scraping over her scalp. Kate smiled grimly and took the road that led towards Newport, scarcely aware of the rain falling heavily on her windscreen.

If it were Debbie in London, staying in her flat for the weekend, it would have been completely different. It would have been fun. Then they'd have been squabbling over whether to have Indian or Chinese and whether the best shops were in Covent Garden or Oxford Street. Sisters. Almost.

But Debbie on the Isle of Wight was another thing altogether. Here she lived the life Kate wanted and could never have. Here it was like looking into a mirror and seeing an alternative universe, one she wasn't eligible to enter. The poor child, standing barefoot in the snow, looking through a frosted window at a family opening presents in front of the fire. Still the outsider looking in.

And it hurt. Still hurt.

Debbie had a husband who loved her. Two children. Both boys. Callum and Daniel.

Kate's heart twisted inside her—as it always did when she thought of how cruel fate had been to her. All she wanted was the simple things in life and yet they'd always eluded her.

She lowered the gear to negotiate a tight bend. She was being selfish. Debbie had lost her mother and was hurting. This wasn't the time to feel envy.

Because it *was* envy. Kate recognised it but felt powerless to do anything about it, even though she knew it twisted and distorted her life.

Six years since she'd done this journey and yet she remembered it perfectly. She knew the ancient oak tree that stood proudly on the corner just before she had to turn left and the old pub on the corner. It was all achingly familiar. Round the next bend was the hotel where they played croquet on a summer afternoon.

And if she could have turned away and run she would have. It hurt. Just being here hurt. Knowing that in a few short minutes she'd be sitting in Debbie's house drinking tea and hearing her children playing somewhere in the house would hurt. Desperately.

She wouldn't take anything away from Debbie. She loved her. It was just she wanted a little of her happiness. She wanted to know what it was like to hold a newborn baby, to feel its soft little body curved into hers and know she was a mother.

Kate took the car past the hotel and on towards Debbie's house. Every day there was this intense pain, a huge sense of loss. A column of ice running the length of her body. It didn't matter that she'd managed to break into a career other people envied, or that she'd bought herself a great flat in Highgate, drove a trendy car. She knew she was a failure. Deep down.

She'd known it when Richard had walked out the door and closed it firmly behind him. He wanted children. Non-negotiable. And if he couldn't have them with her he was going to have them with someone else.

He'd loved her. Of course he'd loved her. He'd told her. Just not enough.

Not enough. His words echoed in her head.

Over two years ago. The fifteenth of January. On a Sunday. From that day on she'd known it wasn't just children she'd never be able to have. It was a *normal* life. The one thing she'd craved since her step-dad had put her in care.

She hadn't been enough for Richard. She wasn't enough on her own—and he'd left. Left her incomplete and hurting.

Two months before she had left for Los Angeles. The opportunity of a lifetime—and one she'd needed to survive. And she had survived.

As had Gideon.

Kate slipped into second gear and rounded the final bend. There was no turning back now. She was here to say goodbye to Aunt Babs. Goodbye and thank you.

CHAPTER TWO

GIDEON decided to wait before collecting his children. Give Debbie time to see Kate before he arrived.

He drove straight past her neat nineteen-fifties semi and down towards the coast. Debbie had been so anxious about whether Kate would be able to make it. He didn't want to intrude. It was bad enough he hadn't got any choice but to accept her help with Tilly and Jemima. It was too much for her.

The seafront car park was completely deserted, which was hardly surprising this early in the year. The rain had started to fall in fat, heavy drops, which meant the walk along the pebble beach he'd have liked to clear his head wasn't really possible.

Instead he switched on the radio and watched the wind catch at the waves. The sea was a fair way out now, but at high tide it would be quite spectacular. Primal. This was just the best place on earth. He couldn't imagine living away from here. All those years he'd spent in cities. People crammed together, rushing around with no time for each other. Look at Kate Simmonds. Somewhere along the line she'd forgotten what was important.

His mind dwelt for a moment on the woman he'd met on the ferry. Possibly she was what he'd expected. She was as carefully turned out as she was on the television, except perhaps her hair was less well groomed. He smiled. On television it fell in a smooth, swinging bob. On balance he preferred it windswept and blown around her face. Made her seem more approachable. More real.

His fingers reached out to re-tune the radio away from the high-pitched woman who was screeching about needing nothing but love. Not much chance of that if she yelled all the time. He flicked through the pre-set channels before settling on the classical one and then laid his head back on the headrest and closed his eyes.

On television Kate seemed commanding and playful. The personification of glossy, successful living. The flesh and blood woman was more confused. *Vulnerable*. That was the word. Katie Simmonds had always been vulnerable.

And beautiful.

He didn't quite know where that thought had come from, but she *was* beautiful. She had a restful, intelligent face. One that came alive because of her eyes.

He remembered her eyes. How they could laugh while the rest of her face was impassive. And how they'd followed him around, devoted. It had been quite unnerving being the object of a teenage crush. He smiled as he wondered whether she remembered.

It certainly wouldn't happen now. Life had moved on for the cosmopolitan Kate Simmonds. She wouldn't give a man like him the time of day. Preoccupied, exhausted and old beyond his years. What was there about him that would interest her in the slightest? God knew why that should bother him, but it did.

Kate felt sick. It was as though she'd been punched hard in the stomach and was left reeling on the floor.

Debbie was pregnant.

Very pregnant.

She lifted her hand and waved at Debbie, who was standing in the doorway, before reaching down into the foot-well for her handbag. It was a chance to hide her face for a second. Give her a moment to school her features into delight.

Why hadn't Debbie warned her? Told her she was expecting a baby, so she could prepare herself?

But she knew why.

Debbie wouldn't have known how to find the words. Not when she knew how much Kate's infertility still hurt her. She brushed a hand over her face and opened the door, pulling her collar up against the rain.

'You'd better make a run for it,' Debbie called into the wind, one hand cradled protectively over her stomach. 'It doesn't look like the rain's going to stop any time soon.'

Kate slammed the door shut and scurried into the house. 'This is vicious weather.'

'You'd better give me your coat. I'll hang it in the utility room to dry,' Debbie offered practically. She waited while Kate unbuttoned it and handed it over before she said, 'We'll bring in your case later.'

'I don't know…Debs, I…' Kate began awkwardly, her eyes drifting to Debbie's distended stomach. 'I think I might be better off staying at your mum's. I don't want to get in the way. I—'

Debbie smiled tearfully and then nodded. 'I know, Kate. I do understand. Particularly with me like this.' She turned and walked through the kitchen to the utility room.

Kate followed her as far as the kitchen and stood with her back against the melamine worktop. *What was the matter with her?* Why couldn't she do this? She'd known since she was twenty-two that she couldn't have children. It wasn't a new discovery.

'I thought you'd say that,' Debbie said, coming back into the room. 'I put fresh sheets over there yesterday afternoon. I just hoped you might be able to.'

Guilt washed over her. 'You know I'm really pleased for you. It's just—'

'Difficult for you,' Debbie finished for her.

Kate tried to smile but it didn't quite work. The corners of her mouth lifted but her breath caught in her throat in a painful lump. *Difficult* didn't even begin to describe how painful she found being around pregnant women and babies.

She'd had six years to become accustomed to the knowledge she'd never have children. Six years since a ruptured appendix had changed her life.

Every moment of that time was ingrained in her mind. She could see Aunt Babs, her round face concerned and supportive, sitting by her bed, and hear Dr Balliol's clipped accent as he told her there'd been only limited damage to one fallopian tube. In itself it wouldn't have been catastrophic. But...

It was the 'but' that had taken away any hope she might have had. The operation had revealed that her ovaries hadn't formed properly. A 'genetic abnormality'. She would never have children.

Never.

At twenty-two she hadn't even realised she wanted children, but the word *never* was a for ever type of word. It meant for all time. It was beyond her control. It was until the day she died. She would *never* have a baby.

Kate looked up and met Debbie's grey eyes. Their

gentle expression told Kate that she remembered too. The memory of that time was never very far away— for either of them. Debbie had been thirteen weeks pregnant. The contrast in destiny between the two of them couldn't have been more marked.

Debbie's hand lay protectively over her tummy. 'It doesn't matter, Kate.'

'It does. I wish…' She trailed off, uncertain what she actually did wish. That things were different? That she wasn't here? That she were stronger and able to accept the things she couldn't change?

Kate hated herself for not being stronger. She could see the exhaustion in Debbie's face. Her eyes were bloodshot and tears were obviously not far from the surface. If there'd ever been a time when she could have paid something back to Debbie for her good-natured acceptance of her into her childhood home, this was it. But…

As though she knew what she'd been thinking, Debbie broke into her thoughts. 'I'm just so glad you're here. I've been half expecting you to telephone to say you wouldn't be able to make it and I don't think I can do this by myself. I miss Mum so much. I keep thinking about how she won't see my baby now.'

Her round face crumpled and Kate forgot herself and reached for her. She wasn't even aware of the baby bump between them.

'It's due in another six weeks. Not long. If she'd just managed to wait…'

'I'm sorry, Debs. I really am,' Kate murmured, stroking her hair. For a few minutes she held her, letting her cry softly into her shoulder.

'I shouldn't be doing this to you,' Debbie said,

pulling away and blowing her nose in a tissue. 'I promised myself I wouldn't do this as soon as you arrived. But I'm just so pleased to see you. I really need you to be here.'

Kate reached out and laid her hand on Debbie's swollen abdomen. 'Why didn't you tell me?' she asked softly. 'About the baby?'

'I didn't know how to. Do you mind very much?'

Beneath Kate's hand she felt a hard kick. She looked up to see Debbie pull a face. 'Did that hurt?'

'Not hurt exactly—but it's not the most comfortable experience. Put that together with the heartburn and swollen ankles; the whole thing's just perfect.'

Kate laughed as she was meant to. To her ears it sounded dutiful but it seemed to satisfy Debbie. 'You should have told me,' she said, pulling her hand away and turning at the sound of the back door opening.

'That'll be Gideon,' Debbie said quickly.

'Is anyone home?'

Debbie reached across to pull a tissue out of a box on the table and blew her nose fiercely. 'I wasn't expecting you for another couple of hours,' she called out. 'I hope you didn't hurry back without getting everything you needed done.'

'All finished.' He smiled across at Kate as she pushed back against the worktop.

'This is Kate. Do you remember her from—?'

Kate cut in quickly, unaccountably embarrassed. 'We met on the ferry.'

'Oh. That was nice. I wasn't sure you'd remember each other,' Debbie said, as she tucked the tissue up her sleeve. 'Kate's not been back to the island much since she left for university. Hardly at all since she started work.'

'No, she hasn't.'

There was a slight edge to his voice that forced Kate to look up at him.

His eyes held a critical expression. But fleetingly so. No sooner had she recognised it than it was gone.

Debbie peered out of the back window. 'Is it still raining out there? Give me your coat, Gideon. It might dry off a bit before you have to leave.'

Gideon shrugged out of his wet jacket but kept hold of it. 'You sit down. I'll put it in the utility room.'

Debbie sank down into a seat. 'I don't know what the matter is with me today. My ankles have puffed up and I feel so tired.'

'Take it easy now, then,' Gideon said, emerging from the small back room Debbie used as a laundry room. 'How have the girls been?'

'Just fine, but I'm afraid Tilly's fallen asleep. Nursery just wore her out today. And Jemima's got a letter from school about an Easter pageant, but she'll show you that.'

'Do you want a cup of tea?' he asked, turning towards the kettle.

'That would be lovely.'

Kate watched, feeling like a spare part in what was obviously an old friendship. 'How long have you looked after Gideon's girls?' she asked, taking the seat opposite Debbie's.

Gideon cut in. 'She's helping me out for a few days.'

Kate swivelled round to look at him. His face was turned away as filled the kettle.

'I'm not doing much,' Debbie said. 'Just picking them up from school and nursery, then hanging on to them until Gideon collects them. I'm Mum's stand-in.'

Debbie rubbed her stomach gently. 'Mum said she'd look after the girls until Gideon's had a chance to find a good replacement for Ingrid. Emily helps too, of course. Rachel Boyle when she gets the chance.'

Gideon opened one of the top cupboards and pulled down the box of teabags. 'Ingrid was our nanny.'

'One day she was there and the next she was gone,' Debbie said, bristling with indignation. 'Very irresponsible to behave like that when you work with children.'

'She's a city girl and found island life a bit claustrophobic. It's not for everyone, living here. I shouldn't have hired her.' Gideon glanced across at Kate. 'She wanted more nightlife than can be found in Newport and my hours didn't help.'

'She knew them when she took the job. It makes me cross.'

It felt strange listening to Gideon and Debbie talking together. In her mind she'd kept everything on the Isle of Wight frozen in time, everything just as it always had been. But things had changed. Friendships had been forged by circumstances she hadn't been a part of. Kate was suddenly aware of a wave of homesickness.

Gideon smiled, the corners of his eyes crinkling. 'Babs stepped in to help.'

'You know Mum...' Debbie tailed off and Kate pushed the box of tissues across the table towards her. Yes, she knew Aunt Babs. She'd never been able to stand by and watch other people struggle when she could do something to help them. Debbie was the same. They were special people.

Debbie smiled a watery smile across the table and took a tissue. 'Thanks. I'm such a mess. I can't seem to stop crying.'

Kate looked at her mottled face and red-rimmed eyes and felt guilty. She hadn't cried yet. Inside her heart was a dull ache, but she hadn't been able to shed a single tear for the woman who'd been so pivotal in her life. Without Aunt Babs she'd have had a very different future.

'It's hardly surprising,' she said awkwardly.

Gideon brought three mugs of tea across to the table as a small tornado burst into the room shouting, 'Daddy! Daddy, you're back!'

Kate felt as though the room had frozen around her. Just for a moment.

This was Gideon and Laura's child.

Jemima.

The baby Laura had been carrying when Kate had first discovered she'd never have children of her own. It had hurt so much to look at the pregnant Laura then. The woman who had everything she'd ever wanted.

That was the last time she'd visited the island. As soon as she'd recovered from her operation, she'd left. Money from Aunt Babs in her pocket and a post-graduate certificate in radio journalism in her hand, she'd turned her face resolutely away from her past and concentrated on the future.

For a time it had been enough.

Gideon pushed back his chair to receive his daughter into his arms. Jemima looked older than her five years, Kate thought, but what did she know about children? Her hair was a sandy brown, much darker than Laura's had been, but her face was the same perfect oval. Beautiful. Her arms flew up to hug her father and Kate felt her heart contract.

There was something so unconditional in the love of a child for a parent. She'd even been like that herself. She'd forgiven her mother for almost anything, grateful for a careless kind word. She couldn't imagine how it would feel to have a warm little figure clinging to you for love and comfort. It must be the most magical feeling.

Across the kitchen table she caught Debbie's eyes and knew she understood. She'd always understood. Like her mother. Kate tried to smile but it slipped slightly.

'This is Jemima,' Gideon said, turning the little girl to face Kate. His strong hands rested on her waist, dark against the pale lilac of her jumper. 'And somewhere around there's Matilda.'

'She's asleep on Auntie Debbie's bed,' Jemima said.

'This is Kate Simmonds. She's Auntie Debbie's sister.'

Kate started at hearing herself described like that. She'd never felt like a sister and yet that was how Debbie always treated her. It wasn't that she didn't want to be, it was just that she couldn't quite accept that she really belonged. That they could really want her.

Jemima looked steadily across the table at her and then smiled. 'I'm five.'

'Yes, I know,' Kate replied a little awkwardly. Why couldn't she do this? After all this time? Somehow in the presence of children she just froze.

'Tilly is three. She's my sister. Did you know my mummy's dead?'

Kate looked helplessly up at Gideon, wondering what she should answer. She'd no experience with this kind of thing. None at all. She avoided contact with children wherever possible. There was no point making herself feel worse about everything.

His face was a blank and Kate turned back to the little girl, who was evidently expecting some kind of reply. 'I know,' she said again, feeling very foolish. And then, 'So's mine.'

'When did she die?'

Kate looked at the almond-shaped eyes of the little girl and saw in them a real interest. Strange. She'd never before thought that inside a child was a person. Perfectly formed and entirely there. The panic inside her started to recede. She could talk to a person. 'When I was eight.'

'I was three,' Jemima said, almost proudly. 'She was very sick.'

'Yes,' Kate agreed, looking helplessly up at Gideon.

He pulled Jemima towards him and lightly kissed the top of her head. 'Why don't you go and get me your book bag? Auntie Debbie says you've got a letter for me.'

Jemima nodded. 'I've got to make an Easter basket.' She ran out of the kitchen without a backward glance.

'She's lovely,' Kate said awkwardly.

Gideon smiled. 'She's a good girl.'

'I'm sorry, I'm not very used to children,' she said, feeling she had to say something to explain her awkwardness.

'You did fine,' Debbie said reassuringly. She turned towards Gideon. 'Kate lives a completely different life from us. She's not a children person. You should see her flat. It's all cream and taupe. Can you just imagine the mess my two would make of it all in no time?'

Gideon leant back in his chair, his legs outstretched under the table. 'Where do you live? Are you based permanently in the States now?'

'LA was a two-year commitment. I live in Highgate,' Kate answered. 'North London.'

He nodded as though he knew it. 'Do you like living in London?'

Kate thought about it. No one ever asked her that. They always assumed she did. How could you not love living in a great city, with fantastic theatres and wonderful restaurants?

But *did* she like it? She wasn't sure any more. She'd been so looking forward to coming back home—to her flat, to see her friends. But when she'd got there it hadn't felt like home. It had just been a flat. Many of her friends had moved on in the two years she'd been away. Had downshifted and taken themselves off to the countryside.

Richard had married.

Surprisingly that hadn't hurt as much as she'd thought it would. It had felt like closure. She looked up and caught Gideon watching her curiously. 'When I get a parking space near my house I do.'

'And do you miss LA?'

'You *must* miss LA,' Debbie cut in. 'Can you imagine anything more exciting than to live in LA? Did you know she interviewed Brad Pitt?'

Kate played with a knot mark on the pine tabletop.

She understood what Debbie was doing. She was even grateful for it. She was to be cast as a career woman. The woman with drive and vision who didn't have time for a home and family. It was how she tried to present herself. It made life easier.

Debbie heaved herself out of the end seat. 'How about I get the children something to eat? It's nearly five. They must be hungry,' she said, turning to Gideon.

'That would be great. Then I can just rush them through the shower when we get home and put them to bed. I've got a mountain of paperwork waiting for me this evening.'

'It's not going to be fancy, but I've got some nice bread from the corner shop, cheese and things.'

Kate drained the last of her drink and pushed the empty mug towards the centre of the table. 'Is there anything you'd like me to do?' she asked.

Gideon had already taken some lettuce from Debbie's fridge and begun to rinse it through under the tap. Completely unpretentious for a world-famous chef. He seemed so completely at home. Far more comfortable than she was in Debbie's home.

Debbie reached up for a cerise plastic salad bowl. 'There's some cucumber in the bottom of the fridge, I think, Gideon. Chop that up and pop it in the salad. Kate, do you want to slice the bread?' She paused and listened to a sudden shout. 'I'm needed, I think. Daniel's at that awful stage where he just won't share.'

She turned and walked out of the room. Alone with Gideon, Kate felt nervous. Illogically so, she reminded herself. The tension was only in her head.

'The bread's in the bread bin,' Gideon remarked.

Kate stood up hurriedly. 'Does Debbie have a board to cut it on?'

'By the toaster,' he replied calmly.

'Oh, right.' She hadn't been to this house before and it certainly showed, Kate thought as she searched in the wrong drawer for the bread knife. Whereas Gideon...

'Debbie has a knife block.'

'Does she?'

Gideon pointed across to the work surface on the other side of the kitchen. Kate walked over and pulled a couple of knives out before she selected the right handle. She turned in time to see him cut the cucumber in sliver-thin slices, his hand moving in a rapid rocking movement. 'Open the cupboard second on the left,' he said without looking up.

'Why?' she asked, looking down at the bread knife.

'There's a basket there you can use for the bread.'

If his intention was to make sure she realised she didn't know what she was doing he was making a fine job of it.

She pulled open the cupboard and found the bread basket exactly as he'd said. 'You seem to know your way around Deb's kitchen,' she said slightly acidly.

'She's one of the few people who ever invite me to lunch.'

'Really?' she asked in spite of herself.

He smiled. It was nothing, but it made Kate catch her breath. He had the kind of smile that lit up his face and made you want to smile back. Foolishly. At seventeen she'd done just that. Had grinned inanely every time he'd deigned to notice her.

'Everyone's intimidated about asking a chef to dinner. What do they cook? Will I criticise?'

Kate swallowed. 'And do you?'

The grooves in his face deepened and Kate found herself smiling back at him. It was like breathing. Completely unconscious. He smiled and she felt good.

'I'll never confess to that.'

'Probably wise,' she returned, turning away and sawing at the loaf she'd found in the bread bin.

He put down his own knife and rested his hand lightly on hers. She looked at him questioningly, her heart hammering against her ribcage. 'Let the knife do the work.'

'Oh,' she said, her eyes transfixed as she looked up at him.

'It's easier.'

Suddenly everything seemed to well up inside her. Coming home, now, after too long away. Aunt Babs being dead. Debbie pregnant.

Something of that must have communicated itself to Gideon because his eyes softened and the pressure on her hand increased. For a moment. And then he moved away. 'It's really important to Debbie you came. I'm sure it was difficult to get away...but it means a lot to her. It was a good decision.'

Kate sniffed. She *never* sniffed, but she did now. Hurriedly she turned her face away and returned all her attention to the task in hand. Just as he'd said, the blade moved through the fresh bread effortlessly.

She caught her trembling lip between her teeth. It had been two long years since she'd felt this aware of a man—and it frightened her. Relationships were pointless. They could lead nowhere. Not for her.

And not with Gideon. That was all in the past. Those dreams belonged to the girl she'd once been.

Before he'd married Laura. Before the ruptured appendix. Before Richard.

'Tell me about your restaurant,' she said, breaking the silence. 'Why did you change the name? What was it before? The Queen Anne?'

Gideon transferred the cucumber to the plastic bowl. 'It's on the quay. Simple as that. We, Laura and I, thought people would remember where it was and it would stick in their minds. There wasn't any great discussion about it. Neither of us particularly liked the old name. There's no record Queen Anne ever stayed there so it seemed rather pointless.' He turned and looked along the shelf, pulling out the balsamic vinegar. 'This will have to do for a dressing. Despite my best efforts I can't get Tilly to eat salad anyway.'

Kate put the bread in the basket and turned to watch him.

His hands tossed the salad. 'The hotel's changed quite a bit since you were last on the island. We now have a restaurant and a brasserie. The brasserie has a limited menu but still uses the same fresh ingredients. The restaurant is more adventurous.'

Kate cast a look across at him. 'And more expensive.'

'Much more expensive,' he said, placing the bowl in the centre of the pine table. He picked up the dirty mugs and moved them to the side by the sink. 'I still plan the menus for the brasserie but I don't cook there any more. Just the restaurant. And I don't work at weekends. Not any more.' He searched the fridge for the cheese. 'I need to be there for the girls.'

'I suppose so.'

'Restaurant hours are long. Laura found it difficult.

After Tilly was born particularly.' His voice was empty of emotion.

Kate didn't know what to say. There was a sudden stillness inside the kitchen. She busied herself putting away the bread board and rinsing the knife under the tap but she still felt uncomfortable.

Such pain. To have loved someone and lost them. So suddenly.

Gideon had only ever looked at Laura. Since the time he'd first arrived on the island. Had never deviated, had never looked elsewhere—and there'd been plenty of opportunities. Kate swallowed the hard lump in the back of her throat. She felt embarrassed by her feelings. She shouldn't be finding him attractive. It felt...

She searched for the word in her head. It felt...wrong. That was it. *Wrong.* Like having feelings for a married man.

Debbie bustled into the kitchen. 'I've put down a large plastic sheet in the middle of the lounge. The children can eat in there,' she pronounced. 'I've got some plastic plates somewhere. If we tell them it's a picnic they'll not mind so much about being cooped up because of the rain. Give us a couple of minutes' peace.'

Kate flicked a glance across at Gideon's profile. The tension that had shown on his face was gone, replaced with calm good humour. But she wasn't fooled. He still suffered. Every day of his life since Laura died he'd been hurting. Doing all the things he had to do, going about his business, pretending he'd moved on...

Had Aunt Babs known that? *Probably.* She'd possessed the rare gift of noticing most things.

'I think the plates are in the bottom cupboard, but I may have stuffed them in the box on the top of the freezer.'

Kate reached down and searched the cupboard Debbie was pointing at. 'These?' she asked, pulling a rainbow of plastic plates out from the shelf.

'Yep, that's them.'

She handed them across to Debbie, who laid them out on the table.

'I think I've got some cold sausages in the fridge.' Debbie pulled a tired hand across her face. 'The kids can finish them up.'

Gideon laid a hand on her arm. 'Take it easy. I'll get them.'

Debbie sank back down in the seat. 'I do feel dreadful. I think I'll get Mike to put the boys to bed, then I'll give myself an early night.' She looked at Kate. 'I'll get you settled into Mum's house first, though—'

Kate cut her off. 'I can do that by myself.'

She shook her head. 'Mum had double glazing put in at the back last summer and the door's really odd. I need to show you how to do the handle.'

Gideon started to put bread, cheese and cold sausages on the children's plates. 'I can do that for you.'

'No, I...' Kate wasn't sure what she wanted to say, but she didn't want Gideon putting himself out like that. Didn't want Debbie to trouble herself either. In fact, the idea of being alone for a while was really appealing.

'Debbie needs to rest.'

His eyes held hers and his calmly stated comment prevented her from saying anything more. It was obviously true and equally obvious to anyone who knew Debbie well that she wouldn't allow her to go alone.

'I'll keep your girls with me, then, until you've settled Kate in. The house feels very strange without Mum in it.'

Gideon picked up three plastic plates and went to carry them through to the lounge. 'We'll talk about that when it's time to go. If Tilly's woken up they might as well come with me.'

Kate gently rubbed at her temples. A small throbbing pain was beginning at the back of her eyes. It didn't matter what arrangements they made for her, she'd had enough and wanted some time alone. Too many emotions were whirring about inside her and she needed time to dissect them all. Understand what she was feeling.

CHAPTER THREE

KATE wasn't sure what she'd expected of her old home. It was still there. Reassuringly solid. The tiny front garden was still neat, with the cotoneaster growing up the north-facing wall.

'I'm sorry to put you out like this,' she began as Gideon joined her.

'Don't let it worry you,' he said, turning his face out of the wind. 'I'm doing it for Debbie. She's exhausted. If she'd looked like that this morning I'd have delayed my visit to the mainland.'

Inwardly Kate cringed. If she'd been a better person she'd have taken over Debbie's boys and sent her to bed. The small voice inside her knew it was true...

'You'd better go in,' Gideon said, nodding at the door.

She reached into the inner pocket of her handbag and pulled out the front door key. It was a dull gold, still attached to the leather keyring Aunt Babs had put on it.

Now she was here she wasn't so sure it was a good idea. The house would be empty. No Aunt Babs cheerfully greeting her. No home-made rock cakes sitting on the side.

Her hand shook and Gideon took the key out of her trembling fingers. 'Are you okay?'

Kate looked up at him. 'I think I've finally realised she's gone.'

He smiled grimly and fitted the key into the lock.

'I'll bring in the box of bits Debbie's put together for you,' he said as the front door swung open. 'Go on in.'

She did as he said, stepping on to the encaustic tiled hallway. Aunt Babs had loved this floor. She'd spent hours on her hands and knees keeping it pristine with some secret mixture of linseed oil and turpentine. Kate let her fingers run along the dado rail. It was all exactly the same. Like walking into a memory.

It was impossible to believe Aunt Babs wouldn't appear from the kitchen, a warm smile of welcome on her face. The house was eerily quiet. No sound of a radio blaring away in the background. Just the steady beat of the old hall clock on the wall.

Kate bent down to pick up the day's post, which was sitting on the 'welcome' hearth mat. She'd take these to Debbie's in the morning. See if they needed to contact anyone. She laid them down on the hall table and walked into the lounge.

A couple of cardboard boxes stood in the centre of the floor, a pile of photograph albums lay on the coffee table. Debbie must have decided it was time to start sorting out her mum's belongings.

Kate took in a sudden intake of breath. It was going to be a difficult job. Painful. Perhaps she could help with that? Maybe she could assuage her conscience by ringing Debbie and offering to make a start on the kitchen cupboards? That would be a horrid job.

Dimly she heard Gideon walk back into the house. She heard his feet on the hard floor of the hallway. 'Kate?'

'In here,' she called back. 'I'm in here.'

She walked slowly over to the dark wood chiffonier and picked up a photograph in a bright silver frame.

It showed Aunt Babs, Debbie and Kate—the three of them. They were sitting under a gnarled apple tree, the trunk so far twisted it had been propped up by a piece of old fencing.

God only knew why Aunt Babs had kept it out all these years. It wasn't a great photo and the apple tree had long since died, blown over in a heavy storm. She couldn't remember what year.

But she remembered the photo being taken. It had not been long after she'd first arrived and she'd been painfully shy. Scared, too. Very uncertain whether she'd be staying for a week or a month.

Kate reached out and traced her finger across Aunt Babs's face. It had never entered her head then that she might be staying for good. That she'd finally found her home.

She felt Gideon move behind her rather than heard him.

'Memories?' he asked after a moment. His voice was deep and rich. Like chocolate.

'Hmm.'

'That's you?'

Kate nodded. 'I was a sad little thing, wasn't I?' she said brightly. Her fringe had still been crooked from the time Bernice Cranborne had cut it with the dressmaking scissors at her last children's home. She'd been an unpleasant girl, but then she'd had an unpleasant start in life. For the first time Kate wondered what had become of Bernice. Whether she'd had any of the opportunities that had come her way.

'May I see?' Gideon took the picture from her fingers and studied it.

Kate glanced across at him and back at Aunt Babs's collection of photographs. Pictures of Robert,

Aunt Babs's late husband, who'd died when he was just thirty-four. Pictures of Debbie, Debbie and Mike, Debbie and the boys.

And her.

Her graduation picture. She was proudly dressed in black cape and mortarboard. A picture of her taken at the Oscars last year in a borrowed dress that had cost as much as she earned in a year. And the black and white studio shot she used for publicity.

'Babs was an amazing woman,' Gideon said, putting the frame back in its original place. 'How many children did she foster?'

'Twenty-eight.' She moved away. 'But I was the last.'

It hit her, quite suddenly, that she had been the *last*. There'd been no one after her. Aunt Babs had said the little bedroom was filled and Kate had stayed. One of the family.

None of the other children she'd fostered had made it into a silver frame on her chiffonier. Just her. Because Aunt Babs had loved her. With that realisation came the full understanding of what she'd lost.

It rolled over her in a great tide of emotion, tearing at her heart and ripping into her mind. The tears welled up in her eyes and her body was racked with uncontrollable sobs. She was, once again, that lonely little girl who'd come to live on the island. Frightened and desperately sad.

'Hey,' Gideon said, coming up behind her. And then his arms closed about her, turning her to rest in the warmth of his body. 'It's all right. It'll be all right.'

It felt so natural to be held there. So companionable. She was no longer alone. His arms held her tightly and his voice gently soothed her. Gradually the painful sobs subsided. She felt his fingers move to push back her damp hair and he looked into her face. His eyes were soft and compassionate.

'She's not here,' she said stupidly.

'No.' Gideon pulled her back into the comfort of his body and just held her. She could hear the beat of his heart. Steady and reassuring.

They stood quietly. There was no need for words. Gradually her sobs subsided and she relaxed into his body.

Gideon hadn't expected this. He'd been prepared to dislike Kate Simmonds. So selfish and self-absorbed, he'd thought her.

Debbie and Laura had been friends. Callum and Jemima were only eight months apart in age. For years he'd heard Laura complain of Kate's selfishness. She'd told him how bravely Debbie had tried to make excuses for Kate's absence at Callum's first birthday party, and every party since.

But…

But the reality wasn't as simple. Her vulnerability touched him. Surprised him. Gideon tightened his arms about her, wanting to ease her pain, protect and comfort her.

Just when that changed he wasn't sure. Her body was warm, her hair soft. The fresh apple blossom scent of her filled his nostrils as he cradled her close.

Beneath his fingers he could feel the silky smoothness of her cashmere coat, still slightly damp from the rain. Perhaps it was her sadness that made it possible for him to feel this way about her? It was a link between them. An unspoken bond?

But she was the wrong person at the wrong time.

She was so lovely it would be easy to lose himself with her. Forget how bleak his life was without Laura. How much he wanted things the way they had been.

It took all his strength not to slide his hand up into her hair. Pull her closer. Kiss her. Make love to her.

Damn it! These feelings had come from nowhere and the unexpectedness of it rocked him.

She was familiar and yet completely unfamiliar. As soon as her brittle control had snapped, something inside him had done the same. With a desperation born of survival he went to move away, gradually pulling back.

She looked faintly bemused, her eyes, wide and childlike. 'I don't cry.' Her fingers dabbed at the wet streaks down her face. 'I never cry. About anything.'

Gideon believed her. One look at her pinched little face in the photograph on the chiffonier had told him that much. She'd been beyond pain. She had the look of one of those mongrel pups in an 'adopt an animal' poster, so badly treated they'd come to expect it. Brown eyes, huge and fearful.

No wonder Babs had fallen for little Katie Simmonds. By the time he'd arrived on the scene she'd been a star pupil, popular, outwardly confident, except…

That look. Deep hurt. Far deeper than words could possibly express. He hadn't understood what it had meant back then. But now…*now* he knew exactly.

Inside the glamorous Kate Simmonds, he realised, there would always be the little Katie. Just a small part of her.

Knowing that, he would never think, or feel, the same about Kate Simmonds again. Next time he saw her reporting from the red carpet, dressed in a

Valentino dress with diamonds in her ears, he'd remember that she was as damaged as he was.

He reached into his pocket for a tissue, but it was empty. 'People you love are worth crying over.'

She made a brave swipe at her face to clear the tears. Her chin rose in determination. 'Perhaps.'

It was a single word but Gideon was aware she'd put the mask back in place. She didn't intend that he should see any of her private emotions again and he was aware of a feeling of regret.

For the first time since the tragedy of Laura's death he wanted…

What?

He abruptly stopped that train of thought. He didn't know what he wanted. It was still too soon. Kate was beautiful. Unquestionably. And this was a purely physical response to a stunning-looking woman. There was no need to try and write a mental thesis on it. Far better to be grateful he was healing.

Kate Simmonds had made different life choices from the ones he'd learnt to consider important. Her life was on a completely different trajectory.

She'd walked away from him. Her manicured hand rested on the folding doors between the front parlour and the back room.

'The chairs are all pushed back in the dining room,' she remarked. 'It makes it look like a doctor's waiting room.'

Gideon thrust his hands deep in his jeans pockets. 'Ready for tomorrow. Debbie's decided to hold the wake here rather than her home. There's more room here and she didn't want to unsettle Dan and Callum.'

'Wake?' Kate walked forward and touched the extended table. Aunt Babs's Sunday best tablecloth lay on top, starched and pristine white. 'I'd forgotten about the wake. It's a strange custom, isn't it? Having to feed people.'

He shrugged. 'It's a focus.'

Kate looked back at him, hearing something in his voice she didn't understand. An edge.

'There's something quite calming about going through a prescribed routine. Keeps your mind focused on something other than having lost someone you love,' he said, answering the unspoken question in her eyes.

He was thinking of another time, another funeral. She knew it as clearly as if he'd said the words.

Kate threw off her coat and placed it across the back of one of the dining chairs. 'You'd better show me how to do the door. I know you want to get back to your children.'

'It's fairly simple.' He walked through the tiny breakfast room and into the kitchen.

Kate followed, ignoring the unusually bare worktops.

'Lift the handle further than you think you should before turning the key. It seems to jam halfway.'

She crossed her arms protectively in front of her. She didn't want him to go. All her strong, hard-won independence seemed to be evaporating. The box of groceries sat on the kitchen worktop ready for unpacking, the door was perfectly straightforward...

There was no reason for Gideon to stay and yet she didn't want to be alone. *Given the choice, she wanted his arms about her.*

'Have you got that?' he asked, looking back at her and then, 'Are you going to be okay?'

She uncrossed her arms and gripped the worktop

behind her. 'Do I need to do anything for the wake? Make sandwiches or something?' *She sounded pathetic.* Her voice was strained. Nervous.

'It's all sorted.' He flashed her another glance. Blatant concern in his ice-blue eyes. 'While we're at the funeral tomorrow some of my team are going to bring over the food. Everyone's keen to stop Debbie overdoing it and we've managed to take most of the work off her.'

Kate bit at the side of her finger. 'Right.'

'You'd better put that stuff away in the fridge,' he said, nodding at the groceries. 'I'll get rid of the boxes in the lounge ready for tomorrow and then I'll be off. Where do you want me to put them?'

She followed him out of the kitchen and stood looking helplessly at the heavy boxes. 'They'd better go upstairs out of the way. There's nowhere down here.'

Wordlessly he picked up the largest. Kate gathered together the photograph albums and followed. The groceries could wait.

'The room at the end,' she instructed.

Gideon pushed open the door with his shoulder. 'In here?'

'Yes.' Kate followed. 'This used to be my room.' She stopped and looked about her. It was charming. Painfully so. Newly wallpapered in soft blue that picked out the blue floral fabric in the hand-sewn patchwork quilt Aunt Babs had made for her. Kate's hand flew up to cover her mouth.

'Steady,' Gideon said, his hand coming up to rest around her shoulders.

Her old teddy bear sat on the pillow just as it had always done. The hand-stitched Bible text was still on the wall. *She'd come home.* But too late. Aunt Babs was no longer here. 'She kept it the same,' she whispered brokenly.

His hand came up to hold her head and he pulled her back into the security of his arms. It was where she wanted to be.

'She always said she kept your room ready for you. Just in case.'

'Except for the wallpaper. I always wanted a blue room but she never had the money...' She trailed off as the tears began to fall again.

'Shh,' Gideon comforted, his fingers smoothing her hair.

She could smell the sea in the fabric of his clothes, fresh and bracing, feel the strength in his arms. And then his lips gently brushed across her right temple.

Kate stopped breathing.

Her stomach did a turn of three hundred and sixty degrees. She turned her face to look at him and their eyes locked. Hers she knew were stunned.

His were...kind. Deeply compassionate.

He raised his hand and gently brushed away the tears from her cheeks. His movements were slow. Deliberate. He pulled her closer and pressed a soft kiss on her eyelid. Her cheek.

Then her lips.

Soft. So soft. Undemanding. Giving comfort.

It was like a beautiful dream. Out of a place of darkness she suddenly felt hope. Finally believed that there was a chink of light for her somewhere. Her future didn't need to be quite so bleak.

Her lips moved under his. She hadn't kissed any-one since Richard. She'd not been held in over two years. Long, lonely years. Had never let anyone close enough.

'Kate.'

He said her name on a breath and his fingers stroked her face. Softly, as though he were committing her to memory.

She opened her eyes. His face was millimetres from hers. His hands moved to rest on her shoulders.

'This isn't a good idea.'

It was like a douche of icy water. She could feel the shock running through the veins in her body. 'No,' she managed, clinging on to her pride.

'You're tired and upset.'

She took herself round to the other side of the narrow single bed. 'Don't worry about it. It's nothing,' she said, pushing up the sleeves of her cashmere jumper. 'Just a kiss.' She looked back at him and tried to smile.

He looked as strained as she did. His hands were back in his jeans pockets. 'I'll get the other box.'

'Thanks.' She nodded.

'No problem.'

He turned and walked out of the room. Kate sat down on the bed. Her legs didn't seem to be working any more, the bones had gone mushy.

Embarrassment didn't touch on how she was feeling. Total mortification came closer. There'd been no resistance in her when he'd kissed her.

He must know that. He must have sensed the way she'd melted into him. She pressed a cold hand against her flushed cheeks before jumping up when she heard his feet on the upper landing.

'Are you sure you can manage?' he asked, putting the second box down.

She turned to face him, her breathing unusually shallow. 'I'll be fine.'

'Then I'll be off.' His hands went back in his jeans pockets. 'Collect the girls from Debbie. Let her get some rest.'

She nodded. 'Thanks.'

'Kate, I—' he began, but she didn't want to hear it.

'I'll see you tomorrow, then. At the funeral.'

She saw him go to speak and then stop. He swallowed and said quietly, 'See you tomorrow.'

His feet echoed on the thin stair carpet and the tiles of the hall. The final click of the front door sounded echoey and over-loud.

Kate walked slowly over to the window and looked down on Aunt Babs's neat narrow strip of garden with eyes that were unseeing. Tomorrow was the funeral. She'd stay that night and be back on the ferry on Wednesday. Not long.

She'd always known that coming back to the island was going to be difficult. Kate brushed a tired hand across her face. It was certainly meeting expectations in that respect.

And Gideon?

Their kiss meant nothing. He'd felt sorry for her and she'd felt sorry for herself. Her arms wrapped unconsciously round her waist. Her tongue skittered across her bottom lip. She could almost taste him.

Well, rejection was nothing knew. She'd survived before. She'd always survive. It had been bred into her.

CHAPTER FOUR

THE funeral had a sense of unreality about it, Kate thought. It was difficult to imagine that the wooden box contained anything of Aunt Babs.

It didn't feel real. Any of it. She was going through the motions. Standing in the right place at the right time, doing and saying all the right things.

She'd managed to do the reading Debbie had asked her to. Her voice had been steady and clear, filling the cavernous church with the words Aunt Babs had wanted said. The details of her funeral had been written out long ago and tucked in the drawer of her bureau.

And all the while Kate had been aware of Debbie quietly sobbing.

But she felt nothing. A strange, all-pervading numbness possessed her. It was as though she'd been anaesthetised against feeling.

Why was that? She knew she was alive. She could see her breath, cold in the March air. Her temples pulsated with a dull thud and her eyes ached. But she hadn't cried. It was all beyond tears somehow.

Everything was happening around her in slow motion, all the colours muted. Kate couldn't even take in who had come to the committal and who had stayed away. A small group, probably just thirty people, huddled around the opening in the ground, Gideon among them.

He was easy to spot. Over six feet tall, he stood head and shoulders above the people round him.

Ashes to ashes, dust to dust.

She heard Debbie crying by her side, saw Mike's arm firmly around his wife. Saw them walk forward and sprinkle mud across the top of the coffin, now deep in the open grave.

Soon it would be her turn.

Gideon stood quietly at the back. His eyes were on Kate. He'd avoided looking at her before. Or tried to. She'd been so strong. Achingly beautiful.

Against the dramatic backdrop of the Norman church, she'd quietly taken her place and read the poem Babs had loved so much. Her voice hadn't faltered. Not once.

Now she stood like a waxwork. All in black, her face ashen pale. She seemed as though she were somewhere far away. Detached from everything that was going on around her. She looked so alone.

But what had changed? Outwardly she appeared calm. A tower of controlled strength. Why was it he could see something different in her? Why could he almost taste her pain?

Perhaps because he shared it?

Being inside the church reminded him of his wedding. It always did. Even the smell of the polish on the pews brought back memories of that day.

It had been happy. The whole church had been festooned with flowers. Each one chosen for its meaning as much as its colour. Laura had loved all that. Had spent hours poring over books, working out the Victorian language of love.

The vicar began to speak. Gideon pushed his hands

into his overcoat pockets. It was acutely painful to hear the words. So final. The last goodbye.

It seemed like such a long time ago he'd stood here burying his Laura. A lifetime. And yet it was just over two years.

Two years of coping. Of keeping his head above water. Focusing on anything but the dull ache that had settled inside him. It had all been such a waste.

Then there was the guilt. The sense of having failed Laura. Of not noticing how serious her condition was. Not having saved her.

He looked up in time to see Kate make her way to the graveside. She was like the shell of a woman, frozen inside.

Did no one else see what he saw? It was as though someone had ripped the curtain that hung across her innermost thoughts and allowed him to see inside her.

No longer did he see her as the ambitious and focused woman who was determined to reach the top of her profession. Instead she was a frightened little girl, wide-eyed and alone. With each step that took her closer to the graveside he was willing her to stay strong.

He watched the tears slowly begin to fill her wide brown eyes and fall softly down her pale cheeks. He didn't know how he moved but suddenly he was there, cutting through the people in front of him.

Kate let the mud fall from her fingers and Gideon's arm was ready to support her. Then he led her away.

She reached inside her coat pocket and pulled out a pristine packet of tissues. Her fingers shook as she struggled to open the top.

'Here, let me,' he said.

Kate gave a shaky laugh. 'My fingers must be cold. They don't seem to work properly.'

'Here.' Gideon passed across a single tissue. He turned away and looked up at black clouds gathering overhead.

Kate blew her nose and tucked the tissue into her coat pocket. 'Thank you. May I?' She held her hand out for the packet.

'Of course,' he said, returning it to her.

'I don't usually cry. Really, I don't.'

'So you told me last time.' His mouth twisted into a smile. 'It's kind of an exceptional situation.'

Kate sniffed. 'All the same, I don't. It's a waste of energy.'

His smile widened. 'Do you want to walk back up to the house?' he asked after a moment. 'It'll give you a moment or two to get yourself together.'

Kate looked around at the assembled people. So many of them were known to her, or had been. She didn't want their sympathy. Didn't want to talk to any of them. 'I think I do.'

It seemed natural to turn away and walk with Gideon towards the path leading out of the cemetery. It shouldn't have. Just last night she'd been in his arms. He'd kissed her. Then he'd pushed her aside.

She glanced across at his profile. He didn't speak. He was just there. Quietly supportive.

Kate pushed her hair back from her face. 'Where are your girls?'

'With Emily Cunningham. Do you know her?'

'We were at school together; she was in my class.'

'So you know her well.'

Kate's heels dipped into the soft mud. 'I've not

spoken to her for years. Not since school.' Or thought about her either, Kate added mentally.

'She's got three children. The youngest is the same age as Tilly.'

Since Kate had discovered she couldn't have children she'd cut this place out of her day-to-day living. And all the people with it.

In the life she'd created for herself she'd surrounded herself with people whose sole focus was their career. The few women who had children didn't talk about them. Far too scared it would affect their career prospects.

She'd done what she had to do to survive. For several years she'd managed to pretend her infertility didn't matter, that she'd never have chosen children anyway...

Only Aunt Babs and Debbie had known different but they were sworn to secrecy. She didn't want people feeling sorry for her. Pitying her.

Then Richard had left.

And the pretence had become harder.

It was as though a red-hot poker had been taken to her gut. Like a pack of cards built into an unsteady structure her life had all come tumbling down around her.

The job in LA had been a lifeline. Her move there had numbed the pain for a time—but ultimately she had known it was still there. Bubbling just beneath the surface.

A chance remark; a pregnant woman in the street; a small mitten left on a garden wall in the hope its young owner would return to claim it. So many little things would suddenly overwhelm her.

'Do you miss the island?' Gideon asked. 'I couldn't imagine leaving here and staying away.'

Kate skirted round a puddle, aware he was watching her closely. 'Sometimes.'

Sometimes she ached for the island. When she'd first arrived she'd thought it was an enchanted place and that feeling had never quite left her.

'Don't you ever hanker after the mainland?' she countered.

He laughed, the glint she remembered from her youth back in his eyes. 'Sometimes,' he echoed. 'When it's the tourist season and you have to drive at a snail's pace to get from one side to the other. Then, I admit, I think fondly of a dual carriageway.'

'I can believe that.'

'But mostly, no. It's a good place to raise children—and I've grown to love the people hereabouts. They've been good to me.'

Kate pulled on her orange leather gloves. 'And if the hotel's going well, there isn't much point in leaving.'

'But for you it's different.'

A statement, not a question, Kate noted. He was right, of course. For her it *was* different, but not for the reasons he might imagine.

'It's a fair point,' he continued. 'If journalism's your passion there's only limited scope in a place like this.'

Kate didn't know what to say. If things had been different she probably wouldn't have left. It was only the discovery of her infertility that had propelled her into a full-blown career in radio journalism and, in time, into television. There'd never been a grand design.

Only Aunt Babs had been privy to that information. It was Aunt Babs who'd found her a place to stay in London with a friend of hers. Aunt Babs who'd funded her while she'd worked as a volunteer at a small independent radio station. Without that she'd never have got her first break.

Gideon broke into her thoughts. 'How old were you when you first came here?'

'Ten.' Kate pulled at the tall grasses growing on the verge.

'And it didn't get into your blood?'

'I had things to do. A world to conquer.'

'You looked younger than ten in the photograph.'

Kate looked across at him.

'The one in the silver frame. That Babs kept out on show,' he clarified.

She glanced away; the muddy path had acquired a fascination for her. 'I was small for my age. I'd been in children's homes off and on since I was three. Did you know that?'

'I'd heard,' he said quietly.

Kate desperately didn't want him to feel sorry for her. Not Gideon. Her voice took on a belligerent edge. 'But they didn't really suit me. I was too introverted. Too quiet, apparently. Not a "natural joiner".'

'Not many people are.'

'No?' She glanced across at him. 'Perhaps not. Anyway, the powers that be decided I was an ideal candidate for fostering out.'

'And you came to Babs.'

'Eventually. People prefer babies. I wasn't especially good-looking either, so that made it harder to place me. It took some time to find somewhere.'

She was saying so little, but Gideon could read the

subtext. In his mind was the photograph on Babs's mahogany chiffonier. The one in the silver frame of a young, intensely serious little girl. It was a new perspective on Kate.

He'd known she wasn't Babs's natural daughter. Someone had told him she'd been adopted—but Debbie had said not. If he was truthful, it had never really interested him before, but now...now it fascinated him. *She* fascinated him.

And that was dangerous. By tomorrow or the next day Kate would be back in London...or LA. Wherever her star took her.

And he'd be here. Trying to keep his life together for his children. Giving them the stability his parents had given him.

Kate Simmonds was a distraction he could do without.

'Anyway,' Kate continued, her voice over-bright. 'After a couple of unsuccessful attempts I landed on Aunt Babs's doorstep and somehow ended up staying.'

'You were lucky.'

Kate paused to look at him. She held his eyes for a moment. 'I know that. Not many people could have managed me.'

He saw the bravery in them. The pride. He admired her for that. She'd had a childhood that could have been his. *Perhaps.* But for a different twist of fate. 'Were you difficult?'

'Hideous. I'd made it a work of art.'

'Really?' he prompted. He didn't want her to stop confiding in him. He had the strangest sensation she didn't talk often about the past. He was flattered—but more than that, he realised. He *wanted* to know.

'The first foster home they sent me to I ran away from.'

'And the second?'

'I was sent to my room for something or other. I was angry.' She glanced up at him, checking his reaction. 'So angry I kicked a hole in the door.'

'Ouch.'

She smiled but it didn't touch her eyes. 'I didn't last the hour there. I was in the hall with my bags packed before I could turn round twice. Can't say I blame them, really. They had other children. Children of their own to look after.'

Gideon pushed an overhanging branch out of the way. He could feel her sense of rejection as though it were something tangible. It pulsated in the air. It made him almost feel angry at the system which had saved him.

It explained so much about the vulnerability he sensed in Kate. When she'd been seventeen he'd thought it the usual neurosis of a teenager.

She'd been beautiful in an untamed, coltish way. Long brown hair and tanned legs. It hadn't occurred to him she'd been so damaged by her past.

No one had spoken about where Katie Simmonds had appeared from. Not then. He simply hadn't known. Perhaps he could have helped her?

Or perhaps not? It probably wouldn't have been wise. Beautiful. Young. Clever. *And infatuated with him.*

Had he been another rejection?

Possibly, he admitted to himself. He'd been embarrassed. She'd been a child. And he hadn't been old enough to deal with the situation well.

But now—now, she wasn't a child. His gut twisted

inside him. She was a fully grown woman and everything about that was making him remember what it had been like to hold a woman. To love a woman.

In fact, it was all too easy to remember what it had been like to hold this one. Her body had been soft and warm. Giving.

He missed that.

He tried to conjure up a picture of Laura in his mind. It usually came easily. Along with an all-pervading sense of regret and guilt. But this time, when he needed her, she was elusive. He could only see Kate. Hurting. Courageous.

She looked down at her feet. Shutting him out. 'Not every childhood is magical, you know. Some of us have to grow up much quicker.'

He didn't want her to shut him out. 'I know.'

'You do?' she asked, looking back up, her brown eyes shimmering with moisture.

'Jemima and Tilly can't have a magical childhood.'

Her mouth moved soundlessly. And then, 'No. I...I didn't think. I'm sorry. I—'

'Things often aren't what they seem.' Gideon felt an overwhelming desire to build a bridge across to her. To make it clear he understood—as much as any person could understand what another person's life had been like. 'My life could have been very different.'

'I know. I'm sorry—'

'I was adopted,' he said quietly. He never talked about it. Thought about it. But he wanted Kate to know.

She stopped still. Her eyes were wide. Questioning. '*You* were?'

'As a baby.' He smiled. 'Can't say I knew much about it. My birth parents were young. Unmarried.'

'Oh.' She started walking again. The wind caught her hair and blew it across her face. She lifted one gloved hand and pushed it away.

Gideon kept pace with her. 'I think my birth mother was only fifteen when I was born. My birth father not much older. I don't really know much about them.'

'Aren't you curious?' she asked, looking sideways up at him. 'I'd have to know who they were.'

He shook his head. 'I was adopted before I knew anything else. My adoptive parents are my mum and dad. They're all I've needed.'

There was silence and then, 'Are they still alive?'

'My dad is. He lives in Kent with my sister.'

'Your—?'

'She was adopted too.' He smiled.

Kate pushed open the gate and waited while he secured it. 'Couldn't your mum have children of her own?'

'Presumably not. She never spoke about it—and I never needed to ask.'

Kate didn't understand that. How could he never have needed to ask? Didn't he feel the same sense of rootlessness? Share the same sense of not belonging?

Glancing up at his face, she could believe he didn't. He walked with his collar up against the cold, his hands in his overcoat pockets. His face was calm.

Nor could she argue that he hadn't experienced any of life's traumas. He had. Life had dealt him the cruellest blow it could when Laura had died so suddenly. *Where was his anger?*

Didn't he look at other families and hate them for having what he couldn't? Or was it just her who felt like that? Had she somehow been twisted and distorted by her life experiences?

She never spoke about her childhood. Not in detail. The memory of it still shamed her. The feeling she'd been to blame because she was unlovable. Aunt Babs had spent years trying to build up her self-esteem, make her believe in herself.

It must be the funeral. The crying. All those emotions whirring around inside her, making her want to talk. She glanced across at Gideon, wondering what he made of what she'd said.

'How did you come to know Aunt Babs so well?' she asked.

Gideon smiled. 'I needed help. When Laura died no one else knew how to speak to me. Babs just quietly moved alongside. Made endless pots of tea and listened. In the early days that's what I really needed.'

'She was good at that.' Kate's hair flicked across her face and she pushed it back. 'I'm going to miss her.'

And you, she thought. Strange when she hadn't thought about him for years. But...

She would miss him. Miss the opportunity to just walk. To talk. To be listened to.

To be held by him.

That had felt so good. The feel of his strong arms about her. So safe. And she wanted that. Wanted him.

He was *adopted*. She hadn't known that about him. What more was there to discover about him? A deep and complex man. Hurting. Lonely, perhaps?

She looked down at the ground as a twig snapped beneath her foot. It was quite possible she'd never see him again. After today. Their lives had touched, just briefly, and then they'd go their separate ways.

She would go back to London and resume her life. Debbie would visit her. She'd build up her freelance career. It would be interesting. Fulfilling.

Everything would be as it should be. There was no point in beginning a relationship when it couldn't lead anywhere. Richard had taught her that.

There was no point in even fantasizing about the possibility of a future with Gideon. He didn't want that. What he was offering was friendship.

She should be grateful for that. Kate looked away, listening to the sound of the wind.

'Have you decided when you're leaving?' Gideon asked, almost as though he had read her mind.

'Tomorrow.' Her eyes skittered back to him, watching his face for…something.

How stupid. A full decade had taught her nothing. Was she really looking for some sign of regret? Because of one kiss? It meant nothing. Not to him.

'I'm catching the ferry tomorrow afternoon,' she said in a stronger voice. 'I'll be back in London by bedtime. Ready for work the following morning.'

'Debbie will be sad.'

'Debbie will be busy,' Kate countered swiftly. They turned the final corner and began to pass the cars parked all along Aunt Babs's road. 'I can't believe how many people have come back to the house. There must be fifteen cars parked along here.'

Gideon let her walk before him up the path. 'People loved Babs.'

'Yes.'

It was a beautiful epitaph, Kate thought. The kind she'd like for herself one day—but the chance of that was quite remote. If she didn't make some changes in her life soon she wouldn't have achieved very much at all.

'Where have you been?' Debbie asked as Kate walked in to the sitting room, her coat already left in the hallway. 'I was getting worried about you.'

'I walked. With Gideon,' she added, turning round to see that he hadn't followed her.

'With Gideon?'

'I needed some time.' Kate looked around the crowded room. 'Before all this. He was being kind. That's all.'

Debbie reached up and stroked her face. 'Nearly over.'

Impulsively Kate leant forward and kissed her cheek. 'Thanks for sharing your mum with me.'

Debbie smiled. Her eyes were still red but she seemed calmer. 'No problem.'

'Do I need to do anything?'

'Not a thing. Gideon arranged for a couple of girls to come over and make all the teas and coffees. We've got nothing to do,' Debbie said, resting her hand protectively on her stomach. And then, as a petite blonde hovered near them, 'Rachel, come and meet Kate again.'

Vaguely, very vaguely, Kate recognised something about the other woman. Her hair hung in soft baby curls. Her eyes were a pale, vacant blue.

Kate smiled, trying to put her at ease. 'Hello. We were at school together, weren't we?'

'Yes.'

Like playing tennis on your own, Kate thought, as the silence stretched. She racked her brain for something else she could say.

Debbie leapt in. 'Rachel lived over by the park. Do you remember? She had a West Highland terrier.'

Kate remembered the dog better than Rachel. It had been just like the ones on the tins for shortbread biscuits. 'Do you still have her? Bessie, wasn't it?'

'No.'

'Oh,' Kate managed, as she wondered which question Rachel was answering. Another silence while she struggled to find a new avenue of conversation. A hand came to rest on her waist and she looked round to see Gideon holding out a cup and saucer.

'I've brought you a cup of tea.'

'Thanks,' Kate said, reaching out to take the drink.

'Rachel.' He nodded at the other woman.

'Hello, Gideon.' Kate looked round, surprised at the blatant adoration in the other woman's voice. Just two words but it was unmistakable. 'Who's looking after your girls while you're here?'

'Emily.' He smiled at Kate, then looked back at Rachel. 'Better get back to the kitchen.'

'Can I help?' Rachel hoiked her handbag higher on her shoulder. 'I could carry some tea through.'

'There's no—'

'It's no trouble. I'd like to help,' she said, giving him no chance to stop her following him.

The insipid Rachel had become an unstoppable force—with Gideon her undoubted quarry. Kate turned back to look at Debbie, her eyebrows slightly raised.

'She's got a terrible crush on him,' Debbie said quietly. 'Rachel's a nursery nurse at the place where Tilly and my Daniel go. She's got a good heart…and she really loves his girls…but it won't do her any good.'

At the far end of the room Kate could see Rachel Boyle collecting some of the discarded plates. 'Isn't he interested?' she asked with a possessiveness that surprised her.

'He's not interested in anyone. It's not just her. There's one or two who wouldn't mind stepping into Laura's shoes. But it won't happen.'

'Why?'

'Gideon won't marry again.'

Kate turned back to look at her, hiding her interest by sipping her tea.

'You remember Laura. She was an amazing woman. Beautiful, clever, kind. An impossible act to follow. I really do believe they were kindred spirits.'

Gideon walked through the door to the dining room carrying a large platter of sandwiches. Kate watched the way Rachel fluttered around him. Saw the way he brushed her aside. As though he didn't notice.

She'd been like that. At seventeen. Desperate for him to notice her—but he hadn't.

Debbie frowned. 'He's still not over her death. Two years and he hasn't looked at anyone else, and I don't think he will. Anyone else would only be second best.' Debbie tucked her arm in Kate's. 'Come on, let's get something to eat.'

Kate let her lead her into the dining end of the long room.

Second best. She'd never want to be that. Even if things were different.

'Ham or chicken?' Debbie broke in on her thoughts. 'They're both mixed in with something else. I think the chicken ones are a bit spicy. Perhaps I'd better stick with the ham.'

'Either,' Kate returned, watching Rachel gaze adoringly up at Gideon as she followed him back to the kitchen.

Gideon Manser was dangerously attractive. It was just as well she was going back to London tomorrow. She'd be much safer when there was a sea dividing them.

CHAPTER FIVE

THIS couldn't be happening, Kate thought as she rushed upstairs to get her car keys. Her suitcase lay half-packed on the bed and her goodbyes had all been said, but the afternoon ferry looked like an impossibility. Debbie's husband had sounded more stressed than she'd ever heard him. It frightened her.

She wasted no time in driving to Debbie's house, taking the narrow bends far too fast. The blue front door opened even before she'd turned off the engine and Mike's expression had her scurrying up the path. 'Is it serious? How's Debbie?'

'Her blood pressure's high. Really high. The GP wants her admitted as soon as possible. Apparently it's the bottom number they're worried about.'

Debbie appeared at the kitchen door. 'I'll be fine. I've just got myself into a bit of a state over Mum's funeral, that's all. They're taking me in as a precaution. I'll be home tomorrow.'

'Let's just get going,' Mike said, car keys in his hand. 'Have you got your bag packed?'

She pointed down at a burgundy case in the corner. 'All done. Oh, except my toothbrush... I'll just go—'

'I'll get it,' Mike cut in.

Kate watched him run up the stairs two at a time before turning back to Debbie. 'What do you want me to do?'

A small frown marred the centre of her forehead.

'I'm so sorry, Kate. I know you've booked your ferry and—'

'Why sorry? This isn't your fault.'

'No, but… It's not that. It's Tilly.'

'Tilly?'

'Matilda Manser. Gideon's youngest. I'm supposed to be looking after her today,' Debbie said, chewing her bottom lip. 'There's no one else I can ask. Would you…look after Tilly?'

Kate wiped her hands on the back of her linen trousers. 'Look after Tilly,' she repeated stupidly.

'Please, Kate. She's not a baby.' Debbie's eyes were worried. 'That makes it easier for you, doesn't it?'

'I don't know anything about children,' she began, and then stopped herself. She was being selfish. Debbie needed her help. She'd never asked anything of her before. Had always understood. Had always made excuses for her.

If she was asking for help now it was because she really needed it. And Kate didn't want to fail her. 'It's fine. I'm sure I'll manage.'

'It shouldn't be for too long, but if Gideon doesn't get back by half past three you'll need to collect Jemima from school. I've rung them to say it'll be you so they're expecting you. You might still make your ferry.'

'Don't be silly. I'm not going anywhere until I know you're okay.'

Debbie smiled. 'You promise?'

Kate nodded.

'What else do I need to tell you?' Debbie reached down to lift a small notebook off the hall table. She paused for a moment as she worked down her list.

'Tilly's folding buggy is in the utility room. Try and make her walk if you can. There's chicken nuggets and chips in the freezer if you need them for lunch.'

Kate tried hard to suppress the rising panic. 'What time will Gideon get back?'

'I don't know, exactly. We've tried to contact him but he's got his mobile switched off. Mike says he'll keep trying but...' She shrugged her shoulders.

'Where's Callum?'

Mike appeared back downstairs and struggled to open Debbie's suitcase to put her toothbrush in. 'Emily's just collected him and taken him back to her house. My mum's on her way across on the catamaran and she'll take both boys across to the mainland with her. She'll get Dan out of school.'

'Can't do that with Gideon's girls, obviously,' Debbie cut in. 'Emily would have them, but she's leaving for Birmingham after lunch.'

'It's fine. Really.'

Debbie tried to smile. 'Liar.' She reached out to put an arm round Kate's waist. 'I'll introduce you to Tilly. She's a nice little thing, but a bit quiet.'

Kate walked with her into the lounge. Tilly sat on the edge of the sofa clutching a soft yellow rabbit. Her little face was serious and her fine hair was sticking up on the top of her head like Mount Vesuvius erupting. It was her hair that made Kate cast a quick glance across at Debbie.

'She's so like Laura.'

'Spitting image,' Debbie agreed, sitting next to the little girl.

Kate stood back and watched. Tilly was a miniature version of her mother. It must hurt Gideon to look at her. Remind him of what he'd lost. Or perhaps it was a comfort? A link with the woman he'd loved?

'Tilly, this is my sister. Her name's Kate.'

Wide blue eyes looked at her. No smile, Kate noted, just serious consideration.

'She's going to look after you until your daddy comes home from work. Is that okay with you? Will you show her where Jemima's school is?'

Very solemnly, Tilly nodded.

Mike, standing behind, was clearly wishing he and Debbie were long gone. His voice interrupted. 'Ready?'

Debbie turned to look at him. 'In a second.' And then back at Tilly. 'Coming to wave me off, sweetheart?'

Again Tilly nodded, the small spurt of hair on the top of her head bouncing. Kate tried to smile in a way that would inspire confidence. If Tilly was nervous about being left with her, then so was she. But surely it couldn't be too difficult to look after a pre-schooler?

Debbie used the side of the sofa to lever herself up. 'I'll ring you,' she said, looking at Kate. 'Let you know what they say at the hospital.'

Kate nodded and stood back to let Debbie go past.

'Oh, I forgot,' Debbie said. 'Tilly can't wipe her own bottom yet, and don't let her stick her head through the banisters. She's got an amazing fascination with that.'

Mike almost pushed his wife out of the door. 'Kate's a grown woman. She'll manage.'

'I'll be fine,' Kate agreed. She felt so stiff and unyielding it was as if she'd got a broom handle stuffed down the back of her dress. She couldn't do this.

She couldn't look after a child. *Gideon's child.* It was like some sick joke.

'Really?' Debbie looked up at her and Kate suddenly noticed how frightened she was. The façade was slipping.

'It's not for long. I'll be fine,' she repeated, forcing her voice to sound confident.

Mike lifted his wife's case and practically forced her out of the door.

But what would Gideon think? His goodbye yesterday had been final. His lips had brushed her cheek and he had turned away without a backward glance.

No regret.

Another rejection. He didn't want her. Not when she was seventeen and not now. He hadn't been affected by the kiss they'd shared.

As Debbie and Mike drove away Kate became aware of a small hand tucked inside hers. Inside her larger one it felt small and soft. As an adult she'd never held the hand of a child before. Had never felt what it was like to have tiny fingers curving round hers.

It was like driving one hundred kilometres an hour straight at a brick wall. The impact was colossal.

'They've gone,' she said inanely.

Tilly nodded. Again that ridiculous little bounce of hair jumping up and down on the top of her head.

God help her! What did she do now? Kate drew a deep breath and shut the door. 'So…'

Tilly just looked at her.

'What would you like to do?'

'Kate?'

Gideon.

The outer kitchen door banged but Kate kept her focus on sliding the oven chips off the baking tray into a shallow dish.

'Kate?' he called again.

Tilly turned an expectant face towards the door.

Kate picked a stray chip off the plastic tablecloth and ate it. 'In here,' she called with her mouth full.

Her stomach was twisting nervously. She busied herself quite pointlessly in an effort to look unconcerned.

Gideon pushed open the door, his coat over his arm. 'I got Mike's message. How's Debbie?'

'They're monitoring her,' Kate replied, carefully drying the fish slice on a teatowel. 'Mike seemed calmer though, which has to be good.'

He walked further into the room. 'What time did they go to the hospital?'

'Ten. Just after.'

'Ten o'clock! That means you...' He brushed his hand through his hair. 'You must have...'

'Been here since then,' she finished for him.

Gideon laid his coat across the back of the end chair, a faint frown on his forehead. 'What time's your ferry?'

'Three.' Her hand automatically stretched out to stroke the top of Tilly's hair. 'It doesn't matter. I'm not going until I've been to see Debs.'

'Ah.'

Kate turned away, reaching into the top cupboard for some tomato sauce. 'Does Tilly like this?' she asked, pulling out the bottle.

'Thank you for...' He broke off. 'Tomato sauce? Yes. Yes, I suppose so.'

Kate turned her attention to the little girl. 'Would you like some of this? You can dip your chips in it.'

Tilly looked at her, wide-eyed, and Kate squeezed a red dollop on the edge of her plate.

'Say thank you, Tilly,' Gideon instructed automatically.

'Th-th-th,' she began, her tiny eyes closed tight in an effort to get the word out.

Kate bent forward and rested her forehead against Tilly's, instinctively trying to calm her, make her feel there was plenty of time.

'Th-thank-oo,' she managed.

'You're welcome,' Kate returned, straightening.

Gideon's eyes were resting on her. Approving. She wiped her hands nervously down the back of her trousers. She rushed to fill the silence. 'What were you supposed to be doing today? Is it important?'

He pulled a hand through his hair. 'I'll manage.'

Kate didn't doubt that. He'd spent the past two years managing. It must have been difficult. Impossibly difficult.

'Would you like a cup of tea, or something?'

Gideon glanced at his wristwatch. She thought he was going to refuse, but then he changed his mind. 'I will. Thanks.'

Gratefully she turned away to fill the beige kettle. Gideon's presence completely filled Debbie's kitchen. Just the simple task of opening the fridge to take out the milk took on epic proportions. Her heart was pounding and her blood zinged in her ears.

She heard his chair scrape on the floor and she turned back to face him. His long fingers were covering his eyes, the lines of his body shouted exhaustion.

'Problem?' she asked.

Gideon looked up. 'Life.'

He forced a smile and the effect of it made her catch her breath.

'That'll do it. Every time.' Kate turned back to pour the boiling water into the teapot, then carried it over to the kitchen table.

He looked up. 'Thanks for looking after Tilly. Did I say that? I meant to.'

Warmth seeped slowly through her body. It had been a long, long time since anyone had ever had a reason to thank her. She'd lived her life for the last few years cocooned in a self-serving desire to succeed. To survive. Had focused on nothing but her career. On reaching the top.

But this was better. This was real.

'You're welcome. I've never spent much time with a child before.' She glanced across at Tilly, who was trying to spear a chicken nugget. 'I enjoyed it. She's lovely.'

And it was true. There was something very special about sitting on a sofa with a tiny doll-like figure curled up next to you. The baby-fine hair brushing your arm.

Tilly had been easy. Helped, no doubt, by Debbie's wide selection of DVDs. 'We watched a cartoon.'

'Debbie said you haven't had much to do with children.'

'No.' Kate stood up and walked back to the worktop to fetch the mugs. 'It's probably brewed by now. Do you need sugar?'

He shook his head. Kate returned to sitting at the head of the table, her back resting against the hard beech slats of Debbie's kitchen chair.

Gideon picked up the teapot and poured tea into the mismatched mugs before turning his head to look at his daughter. 'Finished?'

Tilly had pushed the plate away from her. She nodded, her eyes wide as she looked from one adult to the other.

'Do you want anything else?'

She shook her head.

Kate smiled across at her. 'I think Auntie Debbie has some chocolate biscuits in the tin. Would you like one of those?'

Tilly nodded and Kate got up to fetch one, hesitating with her hand on the lid of the tin. *Perhaps she shouldn't have done that?*

'Is that all right? I'm sorry, I should have asked.'

Gideon was watching her curiously, as though she were a revelation to him. 'I'm just glad you're getting her to eat something. Tilly doesn't like her food much. Picks at it like a bird.'

Again that glow of satisfaction spread through her. It was a feeling that could become addictive. Kate reached her hand into the tin and pulled out a red-wrapped chocolate biscuit. 'This one?'

Tilly smiled. Her face lit up and Kate, watching her, thought she really did know what happiness was now. Then she looked at Tilly's father and realised she'd only just clipped the edge of it.

This was *family*. This was what she'd wanted—all her life.

But it wasn't *her* family. She was play-acting. For a day. Soon she'd be back in London, driving for a future she didn't really want.

And Gideon would be here. Keeping everything together for the people he loved. She wished she could help him. Be with him.

Him.

They had never really gone away—the feelings she had for him. Life had taken over. Richard had come and gone. But Gideon was part of her past. A bitter-sweet memory. An unrequited love and exquisitely painful.

'When you've finished the biscuit, Tilly, we'll go home.'

His words felt like another rejection. But that was stupid. Of course he'd want to take Tilly home. Later they'd go and collect Jemima from school and to-gether they'd all go home. She wasn't part of that.

'What will you do now?' he asked.

Kate looked up from her red china mug with the black and white cow on the side. 'Me? I'll go back to Aunt Babs's house. Wait until Mike tells me I can go and visit Debbie.'

He nodded. 'Will you ring me? Let me know what's happening?

'Of course.' She put her mug down on the table, her hands loosely wrapped round it. 'Can you manage the rest of today?'

Tilly had managed to spread chocolate across her face and Gideon stood up to find some kitchen towel. He moistened it and came back to wipe his daughter's face. 'I'll ring Emily when I get home. I've got to be at the restaurant tonight.'

Kate's eyes flicked up to the kitchen clock. 'She won't be there.'

He glanced across.

'That's why I'm here. Debbie said Emily's husband has got a job interview in Birmingham. Apparently the whole family are going with him to see if they like it.'

Kate watched as Gideon screwed up the kitchen towel into a tight ball, his knuckles white.

'Is that this week?'

She nodded. 'Apparently. She had Debbie's boys until Mike's mum arrived, but she'll be gone by now.'

'I w-want Kate.'

Both adults turned to look at Tilly. She'd clambered down from the chair and was standing facing them, the ridiculous topknot of hair bouncing.

Kate's eyes flicked across to Gideon. 'I could help.' The frown deepened on his forehead and she instinctively backed off. 'If you like. I don't want to get in the way.'

'I couldn't ask you to do that.'

No. Of course he couldn't. Kate picked up her mug and took another sip of tea. The hot liquid stuck in her throat and she had to force it down past the lump of tears gathering there. He seemed happy to leave his children with half the neighbourhood but he couldn't accept her help.

'I—I want Kate,' Tilly reiterated, falling over her stutter.

Surreptitiously Kate glanced across at Gideon. The frown had deepened on his forehead and she wanted so much to smooth out the lines cutting across it. Six years ago those lines hadn't been there.

When she conjured up a picture of the man he'd been back then, she saw him laughing. Always laughing. And she remembered sunshine. Summer and sunshine.

And Laura. Laura in a white linen dress with the

sunlight streaming through the fabric. Laura with Gideon's arm about her. Laura carrying his baby.

How that had hurt.

And she'd run away. Not just because of Laura and her baby. But because Laura and Debbie had been friends. There would have been no escape. And Debbie had happy news of her own.

Dealing with the shock of her infertility, Kate had imagined the two women walking along with their prams. Sitting in the garden while their children played. In such a small community there would have been no escape.

It had been too much. Too difficult to stay to watch. So she'd left. And she'd stayed away.

'Kate's got to go back to London.' He glanced down at his wristwatch. 'Go and find your shoes, Tilly. I'll think of something.'

Tilly turned, her hair bouncing with each step.

'She's very like Laura.'

Again his hand rubbed across his forehead. 'Very.'

'It's the hair,' Kate agreed.

Whatever had made her say that? She really did have the most astounding knack of sticking her enormous foot right in her mouth.

'You know, I can help…if you're stuck. If you need to be at the restaurant tonight.'

She watched the conflicting emotions pass over his face. She wanted to tell him to stop worrying. That it would be all right in the end. But she didn't. She didn't have the right.

And what did she know anyway? She didn't really know how difficult his life had been over the past couple of years. She didn't know what it was like juggling the role of mother and father. How it *felt* to be a solo dad. She was so used to thinking of her life as being less than perfect but this—this was worse.

He'd had perfection within his grasp.

'I couldn't—' Gideon walked across and tossed the rolled up kitchen towel into the bin. 'You've got things to do. Kate, I...'

'Do you have a choice?' She stood up. 'It's just an evening. No problem.'

His eyes rested briefly on her lips before he forced them up to her eyes. *Or was that merely her imagination springing into overdrive?*

'When do you have to be back at work? I thought you had to be back in London by tonight.'

Kate licked her lips nervously. 'I don't.' She saw his frown snap into place. 'Not exactly. It's all flexible. I...I decided to go freelance. My work in the States finished and it was the obvious time to make a change.'

Nice understatement, she thought. 'I'm talking with a magazine about writing a column and—'

'Then why were you going when Debbie needs you?' he asked. His voice was uncompromising. She hadn't expected that. 'She desperately wanted you to stay around until her baby's born.'

The effect was like whiplash. His words stung her. They seemed to have come from nowhere. A sudden distancing of himself. An anger she didn't understand.

And it wasn't fair. *He didn't know.* He didn't know how far she'd come in just being able to take care of his daughter for a handful of hours.

'I think that's between me and Debbie, don't you?'

He shrugged his acceptance. It wasn't satisfying. Kate longed to justify herself. To explain. But she couldn't. Or wouldn't. And did it really make a difference?

'If I don't look after Jemima and Tilly, what are you going to do?'

'Do?' He frowned.

She stood facing Gideon, challenging him to reply. 'I may not be your first choice, but Debbie doesn't think you've got another. That's why I'm here. For Debbie.'

It actually sounded quite good when said out loud. 'You don't have to feel grateful. I'm doing this for Debbie, not you.'

A muscle in the side of his cheek pulsed. Immediately her anger subsided. 'She isn't going to be happy unless she knows the girls are fine and being taken care of.'

'I was out of order.' He shot a hand through his hair. 'I'm sorry. Put it down to not enough sleep.'

'Tell me.'

Kate was an unexpected woman. He'd just been unforgivably rude to her and yet she still wanted to help him. For Debbie's sake. He had to remember that. She had a successful life he couldn't blame her for wanting to return to.

At this moment Kate looked very like the woman from the television. Her hair was a sleek, shiny bob. So smooth he wanted to run his fingers through it to make it rougher.

She was dressed in heavy linen trousers in a shade of rich caramel teamed with a dark chocolate-brown jumper. No one would ever imagine she'd offer to take care of two small children. She looked as if she inhabited a different world. The world of high achievement, of constant change, of buzz and adventure. Which, of course, she did.

But what choice had he? She was offering—and he was desperate.

In the background he could hear the sound of the television being switched back on. The theme tune of a children's cartoon pierced the silence. It broke the tension.

Kate smiled, her soft brown eyes glinting with tentative laughter. What would it be like if she trusted him? Laughed with him?

Gideon pulled a tired hand through his hair and sat back down. 'Anton Filbiere is unwell.'

'And he's…?'

'Head chef at the Quay,' he clarified. 'He's going to be out for at least two weeks. Combine that with a young staff, negotiations on the mainland to get another hotel up and running…'

'I can help.'

Her voice was clear and steady, those intelligent brown eyes challenging. They said, If you don't accept my help you're an idiot. And didn't he know it?

'For tonight. Or longer? Until you find someone else. It seems I'm going to be on the island for a while.'

'No, but…'

'It's your choice. I'm not going to force you. Obviously.' She smiled. Her face was softer than he'd ever seen it. 'What I want is for Debbie to be calm. If that means helping you then I'll help you.'

Put like that it made sense. He watched the way her hair swung.

What was it about Kate that unnerved him so

much? Was it simply that she touched him in a way no one had since Laura had died?

She was so sexy. He didn't know whether he could cope with her around his home even for an evening. Everything she did. The way she moved. The way she spoke. The small break in her voice. The husky note was diluted on the television but in this intimate space it made his blood course through his veins.

Gideon rubbed a hand across his face—as though that would make any difference. Kate was so bloody sexy. It was why he should walk away now. He should tell her, Thanks but no thanks.

If loving Laura had taught him anything it was that love was painful. Relationships were difficult. They took time, effort and sacrifice. And he was too tired to do any of those things. What he wanted—no, needed—from life was order. He wanted things to be stable. Steady.

'Well?'

He looked across at Kate, who was standing with her hand resting on her hip. Kate wasn't stable or steady. She was fireworks. Passion. Energy.

She was *ambitious*. She was no little hometown girl, eager to take on the care of another woman's children. She'd do it for Debbie but it wasn't her lifestyle choice.

'I know I don't know anything about children but I'm reasonably bright.'

He tugged a hand through his hair. 'Kate, I…' It was rare he didn't know what he wanted to say but this was an unusual situation to be in.

How could you be so attracted to someone who didn't share a single aspiration with you? How could he say he was worried about her involvement in his life—however brief—because it was predetermined she'd leave it?

'It's not just this evening. I've got a longer term problem than you can solve. I'm not questioning your ability to look after the girls. It's just that you're not going to want to do it for as long as I'm going to need you to.'

'Surely that's up to me? If I can help for a few days, until I know Debbie's okay… It buys you time, doesn't it? How far along the nanny recruitment route are you? Presumably you started sorting all that when Aunt Babs died?'

He shook his head. 'I've not done anything yet.'

Her eyebrows rose in surprise. It immediately made him feel defensive. 'There are only so many hours in the day and I've run out of them. Babs said to focus on one thing at a time.'

Kate gave a twisted smile as though the same thing had been said to her. Her words confirmed it. 'That sounds like her.'

Her brown eyes looked at him. Wide and beautiful. Very, very beautiful. Did she have any idea of the effect her eyes had on him?

He wasn't ready for this. He didn't want a relationship. He didn't want…

What?

He didn't want what? *Kate?*

That was nonsense. He wanted Kate. He wanted her with the kind of pubescent passion he remembered from his school days. It wasn't rooted and grounded in friendship. He knew nothing about her—except the way she made him feel.

'Have you decided what you want me to do? Do you want my help with the girls or not?'

Gideon straightened his shoulders. Kate was watching. Watching for the slightest sign that would tell her what he was thinking. 'Are you sure you're not needed in London? You didn't plan on staying, I know…'

'I'm not offering to take up the position permanently. I've got a life out there—but I can spare you a few days.'

'What about clothes? If you were going to go home today you won't have brought enough with you.'

She smiled. 'I'll just have to buy some things in Newport. Shame! I'll take any excuse to buy new clothes.'

All of a sudden it was simple. 'If you're sure?'

She nodded, her dark hair swinging.

He swallowed, watching the way it settled back into place because the cut was expensive and superbly done. Her eyelashes were dark against her cheek and then she looked up. Those eyes, dark brown, unfathomably deep and mysterious.

And he heard himself say, 'Thank you.'

She lifted a manicured hand and tucked some hair behind her ear, revealing a diamond shining in her earlobe. She was so far out of his class.

Once maybe. But not now. Not with the baggage he carried.

'That's settled, then,' she said.

CHAPTER SIX

KATE swung the car up the drive of Gideon's home. It was picture-book beautiful. Thatched roof, white wattle and daub walls. A fairytale dream. All it needed was roses around the door and the illusion would be perfect.

It felt like the first day at a new school. For about the hundredth time that afternoon she wondered what the heck she was doing here. She could have sent Debbie a huge bouquet of flowers and returned to the sterile world she'd created for herself in London. It was what she'd always done before. But this time...

This time was different. *She* wanted to be different. It was what handing in her resignation had been all about. The two years she'd spent in LA had taught her something. She'd been a victim all her life but she could change things. Now she was going to strike out and make changes.

But this? This was surely beyond the call of duty.

She pinned a smile to her face and shook back her brown hair before ringing the doorbell.

'Hi.'

They both said it at the same time. Kate stepped back and looked at her shoes, suddenly self-conscious. However much she'd like to pretend she was here for Debbie, she couldn't. Not entirely. She was here for him.

He was so gorgeous. Black jeans, black V-neck sweatshirt and white T-shirt.

'I'm early. Sorry. I—'

Gideon held the door open. 'No. That's great. The sooner I get to the restaurant the better. Come in.' He wiped his hands down the sides of his jeans.

'I can't be late. It's a personality failing,' Kate offered, stepping into the tiny hallway. Gideon was close—and overwhelming.

'Right. Shall I take your coat? Then I'll show you where everything is.' He glanced down at his watch.

Internally, Kate cringed. She was very early. At least half an hour earlier than she need have arrived. But she'd sat clock-watching for the last half an hour. Her nerves were stretched as taut as a bow-string. She couldn't have borne another moment sitting in Aunt Babs's empty house.

She shrugged out of her coat and Gideon hung it on some black wrought-iron coat hooks that looked as if they'd been salvaged from a Victorian school.

'I've been to see Debbie this afternoon.'

Gideon pushed open the latched door to his left, holding it open so she could pass through it. 'How is she doing?'

'Fine, except they can't get her blood pressure down. She's just resting and they're keeping a watch on her.'

Gideon nodded. 'She's in the best place.'

Kate looked about her at the small front parlour. It was the kind of room that hugged you. Dark, because the windows were small, but the walls were painted in a soft cream which reflected all available light. The colour of clotted cream.

The focal point of it all was the open fire. Unlit now, but piles of wood rested in an enormous wicker basket by the side. It looked like something you might find on the front cover of a glossy home magazine.

'I've always loved real fires,' she said, as much for something to say as anything else.

Gideon came and stood behind her. 'I do a great fire, but I'm not so good at cleaning the grate. I don't do it very often because the girls are so young. Come this way. I'll show you around.'

His hand almost made contact as he steered her towards the door which led off the parlour—but it stopped short. As though he were afraid of touching her, Kate thought.

It felt so personal, this. Seeing inside his home. Moving about his things.

'It's a bit of a rabbit warren, I'm afraid. It's been added to so many times nothing inside makes much sense.'

Kate stepped down a small step into what appeared to be a study. A mahogany desk was tucked into a small alcove and looked out on to the side lawn which was dominated by a huge walnut tree. 'How old is the house?'

'The front part here is seventeenth century but most of it is much later. Through here is the family room.' She walked into a square room, painted in a soft shade of yellow. 'The television is fairly straightforward. DVD player is underneath,' he said, pointing. 'And there's a whole selection of DVDs that belong to the children in that cupboard.'

Kate nodded. 'Does Jemima know where everything is?'

'Yep.' He stood looking aimlessly about him. 'That's probably it for in here. Through here is the kitchen.'

Another door, another step. He certainly hadn't been over-exaggerating about the place being a rabbit warren. But every twist and turn only added to its charm. It was the quintessential English country cottage. Impossibly pretty and surely everyone's fantasy. Certainly hers.

All it needed was a dog and a couple of cats curled up in front of a roaring fire for it to be exactly the kind of place she'd pictured herself living in. When she'd believed in 'happy ever after'.

She turned and entered an entirely different space. It was bright, light and enormous. 'Wow.'

Gideon smiled. 'This is new. We had this added about five years ago. I live in here.'

As well he might, Kate thought, looking round at his kitchen. It was a mixture of old, new, functional and homely. She rested her hand on the warm bar of the Aga. 'I don't know how to use one of these.'

'It's not complicated, but there's another oven over there,' he said, pointing to the far side. 'Microwave built in up there. Both the oven and hob are electric. We can't get gas here.'

If she'd thought about it in detail she would have imagined a top chef would put a great deal of thought and effort into his kitchen. But she hadn't thought. She hadn't got past the fact that this was Gideon.

She hadn't thought about his kitchen. But it was all a little overwhelming for a girl who thought she'd triumphed if she heated up a pizza and remembered to remove the polystyrene base.

'What do you want the girls to have for their tea? I don't really know what children eat.'

He strode over to his fridge. It was reminiscent of the enormous ones she'd seen in the States. 'I've made a cottage pie for the three of you. It just needs heating through. For dessert the girls like fromage frais or yoghurt. There's plenty of both in the fridge.'

Kate moved away from the cream Aga and made a show of peering inside the fridge. 'Right. Fromage frais or yoghurt. Should be able to manage that.'

'If you want anything for yourself, just take it. Cook if you like. Whatever.'

Her face must have shown what she thought about that because he quickly added. 'Not a cook, then?'

'Hardly. I see myself as a jar kind of girl.'

He smiled and her stomach did that peculiar thing again. Kind of somersault followed by a belly flop.

'That's a shame.'

'Can't all do what you do,' she retorted with a fairly good show of bravado. 'Without people like me you'd be out of business.'

He smiled. 'I'd better show you the girls' bedrooms. They're upstairs playing with the dolls' house. Or were when I left them.'

Kate walked past him and found herself in a square-shaped dining room. Incredibly formal with a beautiful wooden table taking centre stage.

'This is gorgeous,' she said, stroking the smooth wood.

'Eighteen-thirties or thereabouts,' he said, walking straight past. 'Do you like things like that? I thought Debbie said your flat in London was ultra-modern?'

'It is.' It was all clean lines and easy care. She hadn't made a home for herself. The flat was all part of that sterile life she wanted to break away from.

Gideon's home was a place of memories, of living. A place that said something about the people who lived there.

'I've a weakness for auctions. It's an irresistible draw. I spend a fortune on bringing things across from the mainland. There are some great antique fairs in Sussex which should carry a government health warning.'

'It's beautiful. Old things suit this house,' she said sincerely.

This was the kind of home she'd have loved to have. Although she'd have liked to imagine each item had been carefully handed down from mother to daughter. Generations of the same family lovingly polishing each piece in turn.

'The beams are a bit low up here. You'll probably be all right, though, if you don't bounce on the bed.'

Her wistful mood was broken and she laughed. 'I'll keep that in mind,' she said dryly.

'This is Jemima's room. The girls are here. Kate's arrived,' he announced, pushing open the door.

Kate peered past him. 'Hello.'

The two girls were kneeling up at a four-storey dolls' house. The front was open and miniature wooden furniture was set out inside. Jemima turned round to smile, but Tilly dropped the tiny bed in her hand and ran across the room.

'Hi, sweetheart.' Kate's hand rested softly on her baby-fine hair. 'Is this your dolls' house?'

Tilly shook her head but Jemima answered. 'We share it. Daddy made it.'

'Did you?' She looked across at Gideon. As a child she'd have killed for something as beautiful. It had tiny tiles on the high pitched roof and doors and windows that opened.

'It was their Christmas present.' He smiled, watching his elder daughter arrange a pile of cushions on the sofa. 'It still has all the charm of novelty. Babs made the soft furnishings out of her "bits and bobs" box. I can't lay claim to the curtains.'

Kate walked over and knelt down beside Jemima. Tilly followed.

'This is the blue room,' Jemima began. 'And that's the red bedroom.'

The curtains at the windows hung in small folds and the table in the dining room was covered with a checked tablecloth. Aunt Babs would have loved doing this.

And Gideon had made the house. *A dad who loved his children.* These girls might have lost their mother but they had a father who loved them. It was more than she'd ever had. Life would never be perfect for them but they had a chance to grow up whole. To have the self-esteem she struggled to find for herself.

'Aunt Babs made the cushions. She sewed them.'

Kate's fingers touched the minuscule cushion Jemima offered her. 'That's embroidery. It's beautiful, isn't it?'

'Let me talk to Kate for a minute,' Gideon interrupted. 'I ought to make sure she knows where everything is before I go to the restaurant.'

Kate stood up and followed him out of the room. She looked back at the two of them, their heads close together as they concentrated on their game.

Life might have been hard for Gideon in recent years but he was giving his girls everything he possibly could. And what a room.

Jemima's bedroom was an exquisite little girl's paradise tucked under the eaves, the window peeking out under the thatch. The walls had been washed in a pale pink with a fantastical scene painted on the far wall.

It was of castles, damsels to be rescued and knights of old. Trees twirled their way up to the beams and leaves twisted their way across the ceiling.

It was the kind of place that encouraged your imagination to soar. 'Did you paint all this?'

'No.'

She turned to look at him.

'Laura decorated it. Before Jemima was born. We knew we were expecting a girl.'

'It must have taken hours.' The detail was tremendous. Every leaf showed tiny veins and the bark of the tree held colour upon colour.

A muscle pulsed in Gideon's face, Kate noticed. He always did that when he was emotionally charged.

'It did.' He walked towards the door. 'Tilly's room is across the hall. Less spectacular.'

Tilly's room was less spectacular. It was painted in pale lemon. Pictures from different children's shows had been Blu-tacked to the walls. It was bright and colourful but it lacked the charm of Jemima's palace.

It was sad, Kate thought. Laura presumably had been too ill to do the same for her second daughter. So much love poured into one and so little into the other. Gideon had obviously done his best. The posters were evidence of that, but...

It wasn't enough. Tilly would mind. Sooner or later.

'I keep meaning to do something with it.'

Kate looked at him. His face was closed. Hard. She wanted to put her arms round him and comfort him— as he'd comforted her. Her hand went out but she quickly recalled it. He didn't want that from her.

'Perhaps you could hire someone to do something

similar to Jemima's. I know there are plenty of people in London who do that kind of thing.'

'Yes.'

Kate bit her lip and struggled to think of something neutral to say.

'My room's at the end of the landing. That's Ingrid's old room,' he said, pointing at the door next to it. 'And the family bathroom's to the left of that.'

'Right.' Kate let her eyes follow where he was pointing. 'The girls go to bed at…?'

'Seven. Or seven-thirty. Thereabouts.'

She nodded. 'That's all I need to know, then. I'll do my best.'

'I'm really grateful.' Gideon led the way back down the steep staircase. They stood in the narrow entrance hall.

'Kate.'

She looked up.

'You're right about Tilly's bedroom.'

'It's none of my business,' she shot in quickly.

Gideon's hand reached out to touch her cheek. The feel of his fingers on her skin startled her. Burnt her. Her breath stuck in her throat and her eyes were drawn up to his as though she were a rabbit caught in headlights.

'I try not to think about it. How much love and effort Laura put into making that first nursery. How little went into Tilly's.' His thumb stroked across her cheek. 'It makes me feel guilty because I should have noticed. And I didn't. I was too busy being successful. Off chasing a dream that hardly matters any more.'

Kate went to speak but found she couldn't. Her mouth moved but nothing came out. His hand fell away but his eyes continued to hold hers.

'Every time I walk in there now I see it. Why couldn't I have seen it when I could have done some good? If I'd noticed how ill Laura was becoming.'

'Gideon, I...' Kate began. And then, 'Was she ill for a long time?'

For a moment he said nothing. His eyes flicked back up the staircase and then looked down at his feet. 'I thought you knew.'

Kate swallowed. An almost unbelievable suspicion had started to take hold. 'I—I only heard Laura had died. Debbie rang me. She was crying. She...'

'Laura committed suicide.'

Kate felt as if an alarm had gone off in her head. Sirens blaring, lights flashing. It was unthinkable. Unbelievable. 'Suicide?' she whispered, her voice cracked.

'So you could say she'd been ill for a long time.' Gideon ran a hand through his hair and turned towards the parlour. He walked slowly.

Kate followed. She saw him sit in the chair by the fireplace, his movements slow. He looked battle-weary, as though life had treated him very harshly.

'I thought you knew,' he repeated.

'N-no.'

'Debbie knew. So did Babs.'

'They didn't say.'

Gideon looked up at her. 'It was all kept as quiet as possible. Because of Jemima. I asked them not to say, I—'

'They didn't.' Kate's head was swimming. Her mind was busy piecing together tiny fragments of information. She should have guessed. She should have *known*.

Laura Bannerman had committed suicide. It made sense of so much.

'It was way beyond the usual baby blues,' Gideon stated blandly. 'A very rare form of psychosis.'

The muscle in his cheek pulsed. Kate longed to reach out to touch him but she felt pinned to the spot. She felt helpless.

'I came home to find she'd taken an overdose. There was nothing anyone could do. By the time I got back from the restaurant it was far too late.'

'I'm sorry. I didn't know. I—'

'She was dead. Tilly was asleep upstairs. Only a few months old.' His hand clenched into a fist. 'One day I'm going to have to tell her how her mother died. Why she died. I'll have to tell her I let her mother down.'

'It's not your fault.'

'Yes, it is.'

His words were vehement. Decided.

'Laura was so frightened when she started to become depressed after Tilly was born. So scared she'd slip as far down as she had after Jemima. But I was so busy at the restaurant. So bloody busy.

'Every day, every hour, I live with what happened. She killed herself, Kate. She believed we'd be better off without her and she killed herself. If I'd been home more, spent more time supporting her, maybe she'd still be alive.'

Kate's heart ached at the open agony behind his words. Why hadn't Debbie told her? Or Babs?

Perhaps they had, the small voice in her head whispered. She'd been in LA when Laura had died—so busy with her own troubles. And yet what were they compared to Gideon's?

Perhaps she hadn't listened. Or maybe they'd decided she didn't need to know.

He stood up abruptly. 'I'd better go to work.'

Kate stayed where she was, blocking the door. He stopped in front of her, the expression on his face almost one of impatience.

She laid a tentative hand on his arm and reached up on tiptoe and pressed a light kiss on his cheek. 'You can only do the best you can in the circumstances you find yourself in. Neither you or Laura set out to harm anyone or...' She struggled to find the words. 'It wasn't her fault she was ill. Depression is an illness, you know. Not her fault. Not yours.'

Her own childhood was rearing up to haunt her. 'Neither of you set out to hurt each other or your children.'

There was silence for a moment and then Gideon said, 'Thank you. For that...and for looking after the girls.'

'No problem.'

'I'd better get ready.'

She nodded, moving out of the way.

Gideon walked past. 'Make yourself at home.' He turned and ran up the stairs two at a time.

Kate stood quietly in the doorway. *She'd kissed him.* If she'd been certain he wouldn't see her she'd have howled. Whatever had made her do that?

Okay, so it hadn't been a full-blown kiss on the lips, but...

It had been an unconscious action. Beyond her control. She'd been so concerned about him. His pain.

She'd wanted to hold him. Take away the bleak look in his eyes. She hadn't been in the habit of thinking about other people. How their lives might be worse than hers. But Gideon was different.

No one could deny his wife's tragic suicide was as bad as it got, and the horror of it had cut through her self-pity. Made her see the larger picture.

But was that all?

'I'll be off now.'

Kate jumped at the sound of his voice. Gideon was standing in the doorway. His face was drawn. Exhausted before he started a long evening at the restaurant.

'I'll see you later,' she said.

He nodded and lifted his reefer jacket off the peg. 'I'll be back late.'

'I know.' Kate let her hand rest on the door frame.

He pulled a hand through his hair and then stepped outside. 'Bye, girls.'

Screams from upstairs were followed by the sound of pounding feet. Jemima ran down the stairs, followed by the slower Tilly.

'Wait! Wait!' Jemima called as she flung herself at her father.

Kate watched with emotion as he swung his elder daughter up in his arms and kissed her. Dear God, how she'd wanted that as a child. Had so desperately wanted to be loved.

'Be good for Kate.'

Jemima stepped back and reached for Kate's hand while Tilly kissed their dad goodbye. Kate looked down at their joined hands.

She'd never get used to this. First Tilly, now Jemima. It was incredible. An act of trust. They really believed she'd take care of them. Keep them safe.

Her heart welled up with love for them. *For them.*

And, as she looked at Gideon climbing into his car she realised it was worse than that.

Somehow her adolescent passion for him had mutated. This was no juvenile fantasy. This was real grown-up love. She loved him.

And it was pointless. Kate shut the door and ushered the girls back inside. Debbie's words haunted her. *Second best.* If he married again it would only be second best. Not the love of his life. That was Laura.

Second best. Kate held her hands to her cheeks. She should have run away when she'd the chance. She should have taken a later ferry and talked to Debbie by phone. Instead she'd made the decision to stay and play house.

What was it about her that made her attract everything that would cause her the maximum amount of pain?

The girls had turned and run back up the stairs. Back to their dolls' house, perhaps? She walked back into the front parlour with its open fireplace. Laura's house. She was in Laura's house. Touching Laura's things. Taking care of Laura's children. Coveting Laura's life.

Still. After so many years.

Had it all still been bubbling under the surface without her knowing it? Had she always loved Gideon? So what had Richard been?

It had hurt when he'd left. But maybe what had hurt was *why* he'd left?

Which left her where?

Chasing a dream that had failed her the first time.

CHAPTER SEVEN

GIDEON hesitated before opening the front door. The idea of Kate in his home bothered him.

He'd have liked to believe it was the natural reluctance of a man having to rely on a relative stranger for help—but that was only part of it and he knew it.

Kate bothered him. Really, really bothered him. From the top of her chestnut-brown hair to her designer-shod feet.

'Hello? I'm back,' he called, expecting to see her coming to meet him. But the house was silent.

Throwing both his car and house keys on the oak side table he peered into the lounge. Kate lay curled up on the sofa, her head pillowed on the tapestry cushion Laura had made before she died. It was a strange fusion of past and present.

Gideon walked across, fully intending to wake her, but as he stood by the side of her something stayed his hand. He sat instead on the footstool and watched her. Her hair had fallen across her face and he gently moved the strand from her cheek.

She looked so soft. So vulnerable.

Why did he always think Kate was vulnerable?

She had everything. He'd seen her on the television so many times over the past two years. He'd seen her at the Oscars, looking stunning and confident—he could never have imagined how she would look curled up on his sofa.

Her oversized jumper had fallen from her shoulder

and her collar-bone jutted out, leaving a hollow he would love to kiss. Her feet were crossed at the toes, nails painted in a soft shade of apricot. Those high-heeled designer boots had been discarded and lay carelessly on the floor.

He stood up and thrust his hands in his trouser pockets, uncertain what he should do.

'Kate,' he whispered softly. 'Kate?'

She barely murmured in her sleep but her hand moved to rest against her cheek. Beneath her closed eyelids there were dark smudges which indicated how exhausted she must be.

He hadn't seen a woman sleeping since Laura had died. It felt so intimate watching her. The gentle rise and fall of her breasts, her lips slightly parted.

'Kate?' he tried again, venturing to rest a hand on her shoulder.

Her skin was smooth and soft beneath his fingers.

He glanced across at the clock and wryly pulled a face. It was so late. Despite trying to leave the res-taurant early, he hadn't managed to get away before midnight. He didn't have the heart to disturb her.

And, if he was honest, he was afraid to. Afraid of seeing her eyes open drowsily and look at him. He wouldn't be responsible for his actions then. Everything in him wanted to scoop her up and take her to his bed. Hold her. Make love to her.

He turned resolutely away. Kate had offered to help him look after his children. For Debbie. Nothing more.

Climbing the stairs, he went to check on his girls. Jemima lay sleeping, her hand tucked beneath her chin. As always. It was an image of her he would carry with him all his life. Gideon stroked the hair away from her face and pressed a kiss on her forehead.

'Dad?' she mumbled sleepily.

'Yes?'

'I like Kate.' Her words were almost incomprehensible.

Gideon laid a finger on her lips. 'Go to sleep now.' He paused for a moment and watched her settle back. 'So do I,' he whispered.

So do I.

And he hadn't expected that.

He left her door slightly ajar and crossed the landing to Tilly's bedroom. Her hair lay softly feathered on her pillow. So like Laura's, he thought, crossing to kiss her.

Laura had been so lovely, so full of life. From the first time he'd seen her he'd loved her. She'd been the golden girl of the island. A prize to be won. And he had won her.

But all that was over. She was dead because she'd believed their lives would be better off without her. Not a day went by when he didn't miss what they'd had.

He lifted the sleeping Tilly and laid her straight in her bed. She didn't stir.

The house was so silent. So peaceful. Everyone sleeping. Even Kate.

Kate.

His gut clenched again. Images played across his mind of her curled up on his sofa, her body warm and relaxed. Memories of how she'd felt in his arms, her lips beneath his.

Gideon went to the airing cupboard and pulled out a heavy cream blanket to lay over her. He didn't trust himself to wake her but he couldn't leave her like that. Even so, she'd probably wake with an incredibly stiff neck in the morning She'd be better off upstairs in the spare bedroom, but...

He returned to the lounge and found she was still sleeping. He gripped the blanket tightly.

'Kate?'

She murmured slightly and shifted her sleeping position. Not unlike Jemima, he thought, as her hand moved to cradle her chin. In the soft light of the table lamp her skin appeared translucent, almost ethereal.

He had to stop this. Kate didn't have any kind of future on the island. She belonged in London. Why would she ever be interested in him?

But she was beautiful. So beautiful.

Carefully laying the blanket over the top of her, he turned away and switched off the table lamp by her side. He'd almost made it to the door when her voice stopped him.

'Gideon, is that you?'

Her voice was heavy with sleep and very, very sexy. 'Yes.'

She struggled to sit up, her jumper slipping down further. 'How long have you been back?'

Gideon came back to switch the table lamp back on. 'I'm sorry I'm so late.'

'I fell asleep.' Her hand pushed back her hair. 'I'm so sorry. What time is it?'

'Nearly one.'

'Heavens, I ought to be going back.' And then, confused, 'Did I bring this blanket down?'

'I did. I didn't like to wake you.'

'Oh.' She stood up and folded the blanket. 'Shall I leave it here?'

'Why don't you stay?' He closed his eyes in mortification as the question shot out of his mouth like a bullet. He hadn't meant that the way it sounded—or perhaps he had. Deep in his psyche, wasn't that exactly what he wanted?

'There's a spare room. It's late. It doesn't make sense you driving over to Babs's house.' He thrust his hands in his pockets. 'I should have thought about it before. Offered you the room.'

'I couldn't. I haven't got anything with me.' She looked at him, wide-eyed.

'You can drive over in the morning. It's so late now.' He could see the temptation pass over her face and he pushed home the advantage. 'You're so tired. It's probably not safe for you to drive.'

'I—'

'The bed in the spare room's already made up,' he said in desperation not to make it sound like...hell, like he wanted it to sound.

He pulled a hand through his hair. She was so beautiful. In the soft light of the table lamp her eyes were large and luminous. She suddenly seemed so much shorter. Without her heels she was really quite petite.

'Are you sure? I don't fancy going back to Aunt Babs's house now. It's so cold and lonely.'

'Then stay.'

She looked down at her bare feet. Shyly, he thought.

'Thanks.'

'How were the girls?' He moved across to the butler's tray with its fine assortment of crystal glass decanters.

'No problem.' She pulled her jumper higher on her shoulder. 'The cottage pie was great.'

Gideon watched, mesmerized, as her jumper immediately slipped lower, revealing that tantalising hollow he'd noticed earlier. He swallowed and deliberately looked away. 'I'll tell you the secret.' He poured himself a brandy. He needed one. 'Brandy? Port? Whisky?'

'Brandy would be lovely.' Kate sat back down on the sofa, her long legs encased in cream linen, her hair swinging softly.

He poured her a glass and walked across to pass it to her. 'The secret is…' He broke off and leant close. He loved the smell of apple blossom which must come from her hair. So fresh. 'The secret is to add essence of anchovy.'

'Sorry?'

'To the cottage pie.'

'Sounds disgusting.' Kate laughed. She sipped her brandy. 'Glad I didn't know.'

'Worcester Sauce.'

'Really? Is that what it is?' And then she smiled. The kind of smile that twisted your heart and made it stop beating.

'Have you spoken to Debbie this evening?' he asked quickly.

Kate's fingers spanned the balloon glass. 'She's cross and just wants to go home.'

'And apart from that?'

'Doing well. Just bored because she has to stay in bed. Her blood pressure isn't coming down, but it's not going up either, so that's good. They want to keep the baby from being born for as long as possible. If nothing's changed by thirty-seven weeks they'll induce the birth.'

'Three weeks?'

'Hmm,' she agreed, taking another sip of brandy.

Gideon walked across to the leather club chair by the fireplace and settled himself in it.

'What are you going to do now? It seems Debbie's not in any danger.'

'No.' Her brown eyes flashed above the rim of the glass. 'She isn't. Mike seems much happier but I thought I'd stay.'

'You don't have to do it for me—'

'I'm staying for Debbie,' she cut in quickly. 'I can't leave before Debbie's baby is born. Not now.'

And, strangely, it was true. It still hurt. Desperately. Being with someone who was going to have a baby took every emotion she had and screwed it up into a tight corkscrew. But...

Debbie's face when she'd walked into the hospital that afternoon. *Being needed.*

No one had ever needed her before. She'd always been the charity case. But this time *she* was needed. It was like a cooling balm on the sore places of her life.

And she wanted to be near Gideon.

Like a moth to a flame—or a kamikaze pilot—she was destined for pain and disaster but she couldn't resist the opportunity to be near him. For a time. To store up memories that would have to keep her warm for the rest of her life.

And she wanted to help him, make his life easier. It was a gift she could give him even if she couldn't tell him she loved him.

Gideon lifted his glass of brandy and drank deeply. 'What were you going to do? Back in London?'

Kate thought. Repaint the lounge. Organise her paperwork. Go and talk to her agent. 'Nothing that won't keep. I can e-mail people I need to get in contact with.'

He rubbed a hand across his face. 'I'm tired.'

'Bad evening?'

'Good evening. We were busy. Really busy.' He closed his eyes for a moment. 'I ought to say "I'll manage" but I can't. If you mean it, about helping me out, I'd be grateful. The girls like you, I...'

Like you. Kate finished the words off for him. At seventeen she'd have shaved off her hair to have him say that to her, but now...

Now, it wasn't enough. She wanted more. She wanted him to love her.

She wanted him to experience a cosmic, thunder-crashing type awareness that he couldn't live his life without her in it. That it didn't matter if she couldn't have children because she was enough. Just her.

Kate cradled her brandy glass in her hands. She was really very, very stupid. It wasn't going to happen. He hadn't wanted her when she was seventeen, why would he want her now, when she was damaged beyond repair?

This was only ever going to be a tiny respite from real life. And her real life was work. It was career success. It was London. It was filling her life with all kinds of things that would take the place of family.

Whereas Gideon's life was here. It was with his children...

It was amazing, just being here. *He* was amazing. Just as he'd been at twenty-six, he was now. Only more so. And she was sitting in his lounge, drinking his brandy. You couldn't blame a girl for dreaming.

'What are you going to do about finding a replacement for…Ingrid, wasn't it?'

'I'll contact some agencies. Try and sell island life. I doubt I'd get anyone in under a month, but Emily's back soon. She'll help.'

'Of course.' Kate had forgotten Emily. She was only necessary because Emily was in Birmingham. When she returned she'd be superfluous to requirements.

But she would stay to see Debbie's baby born. That was something. A big leap in her journey of self-improvement. And she would have some memories. She would always know what it was like to spend time with Gideon. It would have to be enough.

Gideon drained the last of his brandy. 'It's time we got some sleep.'

'Yes.'

'Have you finished?'

Kate drained the last of the deep amber liquid. 'Yes.'

Damn it! She had to think of something to say other than yes. She sounded like an idiot.

He stood up and reached for her glass. 'Kate,' he began. 'I'm not good at saying what I feel, but…'

Her heart twisted inside her. 'But?'

'I'm really grateful. I know the whole children scene isn't your thing…but the girls like you and it's really helping me out.'

'You're welcome.' He meant it to be a compliment but it didn't feel like one.

'And for listening to me earlier.' He looked uncomfortable. 'About Laura. I appreciate that.'

Kate didn't know what to say. She couldn't help but remember how cold his cheek had been when she'd kissed him, how rough his stubble. She stood up and put the folded blanket over her arm. 'No problem.'

He paused to switch out the lights before leading the way up the stairs. 'I'm afraid I can't do anything about a toothbrush but I can loan you a T-shirt. If you like?'

'It doesn't matter—' It was on the tip of her tongue to say it didn't matter because she didn't usually sleep in anything. But she stopped short, catching the words before they tumbled out.

'I'll fetch one anyway. Use it or not. Whichever you prefer.'

Kate immediately felt embarrassed. He switched on the landing light and pushed open the door of Ingrid's old bedroom. 'Do you need anything else?'

Kate shook her head. 'A place to sleep is great.' *Being near you is better.* She really hadn't come very far from the adolescent Katie. She was still clutching at straws and pitifully grateful for his attention.

'Right.'

He hesitated at the doorway, looking as if he'd have liked to say something else. She raised an eyebrow but he merely smiled, the grooves on his cheeks deepening, and then he turned and left.

Kate looked round the spare room. It was devoid of any personal touches. Presumably Ingrid had taken everything with her when she'd left. It was just waiting for the new nanny. The person who would care for Gideon's children.

Amazingly she envied them that. They would have a small piece of Gideon's life. It was better than nothing. She snapped off her wristwatch and laid it on the night table before sitting down on the bed.

'Kate?'

She looked at the closed door. 'Yes?' she whispered.

'I've brought you a T-shirt.'

'Th-thanks.'

The door opened and Gideon walked in, holding out a plain blue T-shirt.

Kate hesitated for a second before she took it. 'Thanks.'

'Have you got everything you need?'

She looked round the room. 'I think so.'

'Right,' he said again, hesitated, and left.

Kate ran her fingers across the folded T-shirt. *His*. Worn by him. It felt so intimate. As though, by wearing it, she was going to be surrounded by him. Held by him.

She pulled her jumper over her head and unclipped her bra before slipping on the oversized T-shirt. It was silly. Very juvenile. Really no better than kissing the poster of a pop star. But it felt comforting.

A little piece of him.

She folded her linen trousers and jumper over the back of the small cream sofa and climbed into the old iron bedstead. It was all perfect, she thought as her eyes closed. Just being here.

She was being stupid.

Kate stood at the top of the stairs and listened to the laughter below. It was so *stupid* not to just join them. Instead she was hovering upstairs like some adolescent schoolgirl rather than the professional woman she now was.

Why did it feel so difficult?

It was illogical—and it was *stupid*. She took a deep breath and forced each foot to step down the stairs. She'd managed to walk into A list celebrity parties with less neurosis.

Her mouth felt dry like sawdust and her make-up had sunk deep into her pores. She must look like a complete mess. But that didn't matter. Of course it didn't. She just had to say hello and then she could leave.

Easy.

Except, of course, it wasn't. She pushed the kitchen door open, her heart pounding nervously. Gideon had his back to her but he still managed to exude sex appeal. His hair was still damp from his morning shower and his jeans revealed what an athlete he was.

He stood at the Aga, stirring something in a heavy cast-iron frying pan. Jemima was doing a forward roll and Tilly was sucking a tassel on the checked cushion.

With one cursory glance, Kate took in the whole picture.

'Hello,' she said, letting go of the door handle. 'Have I overslept?'

Gideon turned round. His smile was welcoming and inclusive. Kate could feel her stomach do the normal fandango it did around him, but she resisted the temptation to run her fingers through her hair. It wouldn't make any difference to the lack of make-up. She'd still look a mess. And he'd still look gorgeous.

'You're a couple hours behind Tilly, but nothing a sensible adult wouldn't call normal.'

She found her mouth twisted into the inane grin it

also always did around him. 'What time does she wake?'

'Six, if I'm lucky. If the clock still shows five-something I feel a bit hard done by.'

No wonder he looked so tired. His lifestyle was punishing. Going to bed after midnight and getting up before the lark—almost. 'I suppose I'd better be off. Get out of your way.'

'Stay and have some breakfast.'

'Daddy's doing scrambled egg,' Jemima said, standing up. 'He puts cream in it.'

Kate glanced across at Gideon. His eyes were glinting mischievously. 'The cream's not obligatory if the calorie count's too high.'

'Not to mention the cholesterol,' Kate returned, forgetting for a moment how awkward she felt. 'I don't want to get in the way. You're busy. This is your family time.'

'Sit down,' Gideon instructed. 'At least have some coffee. What do you normally have for breakfast?'

The smell of toast was irresistible.

Breakfast. Kate could almost remember the days when she'd eaten breakfast. 'Coffee and toast would be great.'

'Just toast. With butter?'

She was about to say no when she caught the glint in his eye. It had been such a long time since she'd been teased. By anyone.

Aunt Babs hadn't had that sort of sense of humour, and Debbie was always so careful round her, fearful of hurting her feelings. Work colleagues wouldn't dare. Friends? Did she really have friends?

Kate wondered. Over the past couple of years she'd pushed people away. She hadn't wanted their sympathy. And then, so many of her friends had been Richard's too. It had made things…difficult.

'Butter would be great.' *What the hell?* Live dangerously. It was worth it for the look of surprise in Gideon's eyes.

He put the scrambled eggs into a bowl and placed it in the centre of the table. They were perfect. Just the right amount of runniness and an obvious creamy texture.

'Jemima, sit down.'

Jemima ignored him. She was doing a pirouette. 'Are you taking me to school today, Kate?' she wanted to know.

Kate glanced across at Gideon.

'Sit down,' he repeated. 'I'm taking you to school—but not until you've eaten your breakfast.'

'I want to sit next to Kate,' she said belligerently.

Only then did Kate notice that Tilly had taken the seat next to her, her limpid eyes watching her closely.

Gideon glanced across at her, his expression clearly one of mute apology. 'You can sit next to Kate if you sit at the end of the table.'

Jemima's face started to crumple. 'I want to sit next to Kate.'

'I could sit at the end,' Kate said hurriedly. 'Then you'd both be next to me.' She stood up and shuffled round the table to take the chair at the end. 'Is that better?'

Jemima nodded. 'Can I have tomato sauce on my eggs?'

'If you must,' Gideon responded dryly.

Kate looked up and again met his eyes. She wasn't used to this. *Friendship.* That was what it felt like. *Family.*

Either way, she wasn't used to it.

He slotted the hot toast into a toast rack in the centre of the table. Each slice had been cut in half. 'Very cheffy,' she remarked, letting her eyes twinkle.

'I hate bendy toast,' he said, taking the seat opposite her. 'Might as well do it properly.'

Kate reached out for a slice and recklessly smeared it with butter.

'Are you coming with Daddy and me to school?' Jemima asked with all the tenacity of a child.

'Kate's busy,' Gideon answered.

To the left of her, little Tilly was struggling to manage her toast. She pushed her plate towards Kate.

'She wants you to cut it,' Gideon said apologetically.

'Do you?' Kate asked her.

Tilly nodded.

Kate took Tilly's knife and fork and cut the toast into long fingers. 'Is that enough?'

Tilly shook her head.

'She wants it in squares,' Jemima cut in.

Tilly nodded solemnly.

Kate turned the plate and cut across the toast to make neat squares. 'There.'

Tilly nodded and Jemima spoke for her. 'She means thank you. She doesn't like to speak.'

'Eat your breakfast,' Gideon said firmly.

Kate bit into her toast.

'I'll get you your coffee now,' he said, standing. 'Are you going to see Debbie this morning?'

'Yes. Mike's going to work and I'm being allowed to visit in his place. A special dispensation. I promised I'd take her in something to do. I'm not sure

Mike approves, but she wants to start going through her mum's paperwork.'

Gideon passed her a cream mug. The rich aroma of fine coffee just added to the intoxication of being there. She would never smell freshly ground coffee beans again without thinking of Gideon and how it felt to be included in his inner circle.

'It doesn't sound like a good idea. If the point of her being given bedrest is to make her take things easy.'

'Debbie has to be busy. She's going to be more stressed by knowing it's all sitting in boxes not being done than by quietly working through it all.'

His mouth twisted. 'Like mother, like daughter.'

Kate smiled. 'They're very similar. I've got her to agree to let me start on the cupboards. I'm going to clear out everything I know isn't valuable or personal. Give it to charity.'

'I've got to bring in something beginning with F,' Jemima interrupted, obviously irritated at being ignored.

Kate put down her mug and concentrated. 'F.'

'And I can't think of anything!'

'Beginning with F?'

'Yes.'

Gideon poured Tilly another glass of milk. 'They take an object into school beginning with the letter of the week. It goes on the showing table.'

'And this week is F. I get it.' Kate looked at Jemima. 'What about fox? Or football?'

'Anastasia brought in a fox and Mrs Barker said she doesn't want footballs because they bounce.'

'Oh,' Kate said, eating the last of her toast.

'You don't have to take anything,' Gideon said.

'But I want to.'

'What about fish?'

'Fish is good.' Kate smiled at Jemima. 'Why don't you take in that book about the fish with the beautiful scales? The one I read to you yesterday? That's a lovely book.'

Jemima's eyes brightened and Gideon whispered, 'Inspired.'

A glow of satisfaction like she'd never known spread over Kate. It was as if she'd won a major journalistic award. Instead she'd managed to answer a five-year-old satisfactorily. *Very strange.*

This was what she wanted. Kate felt her heart swell with emotion. This was what she'd missed. All her life.

She'd never known what it was like to be part of a family. Even when her mother was alive—it just hadn't been like this.

Her mother had been an alcoholic. The only thing she'd ever really been aware of was the desperate need for another drink. It was always going to be her last. Always.

Even at seven, Kate had known it wasn't going to happen. She still remembered the shame she'd felt when her mum had fallen in a drunken stupor in the hall of their terraced house. She'd tried to stand in front of her so the neighbours wouldn't see.

She took another sip of coffee. This was another world. A different life.

'Have you finished?' Gideon asked his elder daughter.

'Yes.'

'Then go and get your book bag. I'll sign your reading record.'

Jemima climbed down from her chair and ran out of the kitchen.

'It doesn't stop, does it?' Kate remarked. 'Your life is exhausting.'

Gideon smiled. 'It was smoother when Ingrid was here.'

'I l-l-like K-Kate,' Tilly managed.

Automatically, Kate reached out and stroked her fine hair. 'I like you too, sweetheart.'

Tilly caught her hand—and then she stood up and threw her small arms around Kate's neck. It was a perfect kiss. Almost. Her lips nearly formed the correct shape but the effect was electric.

Kate wrapped her arms around the small figure and hugged her back. She'd never been kissed by a child. *Never.*

And she would never forget it.

'Tilly, can you bring me your shoes?'

The little girl turned and ran out of the room.

'Sorry,' Gideon said. 'I hope her kiss wasn't too sticky. Not exactly what you're used to first thing in the morning, is it?'

Kate swallowed. 'Not what I'm used to at all.'

He smiled. He hadn't understood. How could he? He had no idea what that embrace had meant to her. It felt as if she'd splintered. Like a block of ice, suddenly splintered. Not painful. Releasing.

Jemima burst through the door. 'I've found my fish book. Will you take me to school, Kate?'

'Jemima,' Gideon cautioned.

'I can. If you like…' Kate tailed off, suddenly worried she was intruding. Just because the girls wanted her didn't mean he did.

Gideon merely shrugged. 'Have you got your reading record book?'

'It's in my bag,' Jemima replied.

'Go and get it.'

'Is Tilly at Nursery this morning?'

Gideon stood up and began to stack the dishwasher. 'She finishes at twelve.'

'Will they know it's going to be me?'

Gideon stopped and turned to face her, plate in hand. 'Kate, I…' And then, 'Are you sure about this? It's not your problem.'

'It's fine. I'm going to be here so I might as well be useful.'

He put the plate in the dishwasher rack. 'Why don't you get some things together and stay here?'

And Kate wanted to. She was aware of an overwhelming need to be part of this family. Of wanting to stay with Tilly. And with Jemima.

And with Gideon.

'Why don't you collect your things from Babs's house. It can't be nice staying there without her. Jemima's at school all day. Tilly's out all morning. You'd have some time to work.' He stopped himself, as though he'd suddenly realised what he was asking.

'That would be great.' The words had come from her mouth but Kate didn't quite know how. 'There's not much to collect, though. I'll need to go and buy a few things.'

His hand rubbed at the back of his neck. 'I forgot that.'

'Maybe I could go this afternoon, after Tilly's finished at nursery. Would that be okay?'

'Of course.'

Kate knew it was stupid, but she couldn't resist the

opportunity to share his life. She was going to be hurt when it was time to leave, but it would hurt to leave now. It was already too late to avoid that.

And the immediate alternative was irresistible.

CHAPTER EIGHT

'WHAT are you doing?'

Kate looked up as Gideon stood in the doorway. Even after ten days it still sent a shiver of appreciation whooshing down her spine when he arrived home.

'Making an Easter basket.' She pushed the arrangement towards the centre of the table. 'What does it look like?'

He flung his coat down over the side of the sofa. 'Truthfully?'

She nodded.

'A mess.' His blue eyes glinted across at her.

Kate looked critically at the papier-mâché basket and pulled a face. 'Jemima needs one for next Friday. We found a picture in a book and I was trying to copy it. It's not very good, is it?'

'It might be better when it dries.'

'Do you think?'

'No.' He smiled. 'Not really.'

She stood up and went to wash her hands. 'It might be better when it's painted.'

'It might,' he agreed.

Kate swung round to look at him. 'You're laughing at me.'

'Just a little. Do you mind?'

'At least I'm trying.'

His face sobered. 'I know.'

'It really matters to Jemima, you know. She needs to take it in because they're going to practise carrying them.' Kate reached for a towel to dry her hands on. 'I know I'm not really good at this kind of thing—'

'Do you know what the time is?' he asked, coming further into the room.

Kate glanced up at the old school clock. It was past one. 'Late.'

It made no difference, though. She would always be sitting up waiting for him. This was the highlight of her day. As much as she loved being with the girls, this was the perfect time. The part when he came back from the restaurant and she was there for him. Just the two of them.

She pulled a face as she looked down at the disaster she'd created. 'Do you have any idea how hard it is to make daffodils out of paper?'

He laughed. 'How long have you been trying?'

'You don't want to know. Too long.'

Gideon sat on the seat and pulled the basket towards him. 'I think you need a stronger structure. Have you got any more chicken wire?'

'Here,' Kate said, passing across a small roll. 'The clippers are in the box.'

She watched as he clipped a narrow strip and began to reinforce the handle. Then he began to wrap glue-sodden newspaper round it. 'If I cover it with a couple of layers we can leave it to dry overnight. Add some more over the weekend.'

'And the daffodils?'

His eyes glinted up at her. Completely sinful. 'Past saving. Perhaps we'd better get some tissue paper and you can see if you're more gifted with chrysanthemums.'

Definitely worth staying up for.

'We had an amazing night at the restaurant,' he

continued, wrapping a final piece of newspaper round the handle. 'There was a party of three in. All strangers to the island. I just wonder whether they might be from Michelin. They ordered such a wide selection.'

And then he smiled. 'They're probably not. I've started to see them everywhere.'

'But it went well?'

'As near perfect as it's possible to get.' He smiled, standing up to wash his hands under the tap. 'I'd forgotten how much I missed this. Someone to talk to at the end of a long day.'

Kate busied herself with putting away all the scraps of paper. 'Me too.'

'Have you always lived alone? Since you left university?'

She wiped the kitchen table. 'Not always.'

Gideon stood with his back to the kitchen sink, his eyebrow raised.

'I lived with a reporter called Richard Tillsbury.' She shrugged. 'For just over three years.'

'And?'

She gave the table a final wipe. 'And now I don't.'

'Your decision or his?'

Kate stood up straight. 'He left me. Then I went to LA.'

'Have you seen him since you've been back?'

'Unavoidable. He's married to a colleague of mine, Amanda Dallamine.' She walked over to the bin to throw the glue-clogged cloth away.

He watched her thoughtfully. 'Was he responsible for the change of career direction?'

Kate turned.

Was he?

No. Actually, he wasn't. The dissatisfaction had

been there before; it was just that she hadn't allowed herself to think about it.

During all her time with Richard she'd been busy lying to herself. Trying to convince herself that all was well and that if she couldn't have it all, she *did* have enough. That she wanted the high-pressure career that seemed to be within her grasp.

'No,' she said at last. 'I think living in LA for two years was. It was a fantastic experience, in lots of ways, and I wouldn't want to have missed it for anything, but...'

'But?'

'It gave me the opportunity to discover some things about myself. I like television but I prefer radio. I love radio but I want to try writing.' She shrugged. 'That kind of thing. I'm really excited by the idea of writing my own magazine column. Doing something different.'

Gideon smiled.

Something different. But not so different that she'd give up her exciting life for him. Such energy and enthusiasm. Always chasing the next big thing. He would be fooling himself if he ever thought she'd settle for the little he could offer.

Twelve days since she'd arrived on the island and his life had changed beyond recognition. He wouldn't have believed it possible.

She turned her head and caught him watching her. He spun round and opened the fridge. 'I put a nice white in here earlier. Would you like a glass?'

'That would be lovely.'

'Go through to the lounge. I'll bring it through.'

She nodded and he couldn't resist watching her

walk away. That oh, so feminine sway of the hips. Her long, long legs poured into figure-hugging jeans.

He concentrated on opening the bottle and took down a couple of glasses from a high shelf. *This was madness.* He shouldn't be seeking her company. It would only make the inevitable parting more painful. She *would* leave the island and he would miss her.

In the ten days she'd shared his home she'd brought life back into it. Subtle changes had started to occur. Simple things she probably wasn't even aware he'd noticed.

But he had. He'd noticed the way she'd Blu-tacked Jemima's paintings on the kitchen door and the pink heart-shaped cushion she'd bought for Tilly's bedroom.

He couldn't miss the way she stayed up until he was home, ready to talk or disappear depending on his mood. Always ready to fill him in on the things he'd missed with his girls.

Like tonight. Past one in the morning. She'd still been awake. She'd even lit a fire in the parlour grate, which filled the space with a sense of homecoming.

She sat on the sofa, a cushion hugged against her. In the subdued light her face seemed more angular, more mysterious, her cheekbones clearly defined and her eyes enormous.

He would miss this.

'This is always the hardest time of day,' he said, passing over a glass. 'After Laura died, during the day I'm too busy to think about anything much, but in the evening, after work…'

Kate sipped the chilled alcohol and waited.

'When you shut the door, basically you're alone. Do you know what I mean?'

Kate nodded. She understood. It wasn't the same for her but she knew how she'd felt when Richard left. For three years she'd been part of a couple and then suddenly she wasn't.

Rejected, bruised, suddenly responsible for all the bills, dealing with every aspect of her life alone. How much worse must it have been for Gideon?

The light from the fire played on his face and she sat listening to the sound of the flames crackling.

'In the first few months I didn't think I'd manage to get through it.'

Kate curled up tighter and watched him. She could see so many thoughts passing across his handsome face. 'But you did,' she said quietly. 'You've kept everything together.'

'With help.' He nodded, sipping his own wine. 'Babs was amazing. In those very early days she often stayed up late until I got back from the restaurant. Put the girls to bed, read them stories. Like you.'

'She'd a natural empathy with loss, I think,' Kate said slowly, her words pooling in the quiet. 'She was so young when she was widowed.'

Gideon moved to sit next to her and sat back in the opposite corner. 'Robert?'

'He died when she was only twenty-eight. She filled her life with people who needed her. People like me,' Kate said quietly.

He was watching her closely. 'I can't imagine what it's like to suddenly go and live with strangers. I was lucky to be adopted so young. I don't think I've fully appreciated that before.'

'Starting at a new school was the hardest.' Kate took another sip of wine.

This was strangely cathartic. An unburdening of oneself in the quiet of the night. Intimate and private.

'I hated going to a new school. Having no friends, often wearing the wrong uniform.'

'When were you put into care?'

She looked up at him, searching for revulsion in his face. It didn't matter how many times she told herself her background wasn't her fault, she'd never quite believed it. Somehow she must have been to blame, done something to warrant such a pitiful start.

Richard hadn't liked it at all. His family had connections, knew the right people. Had money and influence. All of that had been important to him. During their time together he'd insisted she didn't talk about it. He certainly didn't want his parents to know. They had higher aspirations for their only son.

'Seven and a half. Permanently, that is. Before that I'd been in and out for odd weeks. Whenever my mother was completely unable to take care of me. She was an alcoholic.'

She looked up, searching for the inevitable repulsion, but she didn't find it. In its place was a gentle understanding; compassion would be a better word.

'And you still drink? I'd have thought you wouldn't be able to bear the stuff.'

She glanced down at the liquid in her hand. 'Not often and never alone.'

'Sounds sensible,' he said softly, his eyes still intently watching her.

Kate looked back up. 'From the age of ten I lived with Aunt Babs and got used to her small glass of sherry on a Sunday evening. It took the fear away.'

He reached out and gently touched her face. Kate could scarcely breathe. She should have pulled away, stopped the contact. Where was her sense of self-preservation?

His hand fell away but his eyes still watched her and they were like a caress. 'You're an amazing woman, Kate Simmonds.'

'I don't think my mother liked alcohol much,' she rushed on, uncomfortable with the compliment but loving it at the same time. 'I think she drank to forget. Whenever life got too difficult. When a new boyfriend finished with her, that kind of thing.'

He nodded. 'And she died when you were eight. That's a tough start.'

'How did you know that?' She looked up, surprised.

'You told Jemima. That first day. In Debbie's kitchen.'

Kate wanted to hide her face. She felt so exposed, so open to him. It was risky. It was terrifying. It was exhilarating. So many emotions rushed through her like a lava flow.

'I'm surprised you remembered that.'

'I remembered.'

Kate felt the blood rush to her face. She hurriedly looked away and sipped her wine.

'That's one of the reasons why Jemima likes you so much. Most adults can't cope with her saying her mum died. They get flustered and tend to pretend they haven't heard her. But you…you told her you knew how that felt. I don't think that's ever happened to her before.'

A warm glow spread through her as she listened to his words. Even when she'd felt most awkward, most uncomfortable, she'd managed to do something right.

'And then there's Tilly. She's begun to talk to you.

Trust you. You're not embarrassed by her stutter. You give her time.'

Kate smiled. 'And stop Jemima from speaking for her.'

'That too.' His eyes laughed and then sobered. 'For someone who doesn't like children, you've done an amazing job.'

He stood up and added another log to the fire, waiting by it as the sparks flew up.

Kate drained her glass.

Gideon picked up the bottle. 'More?'

She shook her head. 'No. I probably ought to go to bed.'

'It is late,' he said, glancing down at his watch. 'Kate…' He crossed back to sit beside her on the sofa. 'Are you busy tomorrow evening?'

She watched the flames flare up and settle down before she registered what he'd asked. She turned to look at him. 'Do you need to go to the restaurant? I've got nothing planned. I could look after the girls for you.'

'No.' His eyes were on the pale liquid in his glass. He seemed unaccountably nervous. If she'd been interviewing him she'd have been at pains to put him at his ease.

As it was, she just watched him.

'That's not what I mean.' Another pause and then, 'The girls are sleeping over at Emily and Russell's. It's been arranged for weeks.' He shifted uncomfortably. 'It's a party at the village hall. Harriet and Andrew's tenth wedding anniversary. Do you remember them?'

Kate remembered. They'd been part of the golden

circle. The beautiful people who'd surrounded Gideon's Laura.

She nodded, uncertain what to say. Not really sure what she was feeling.

'Will you come with me?' His voice was low.

Kate settled her empty glass down on the side. *As a friend? Or as a date?* It was a question she couldn't ask him. Perhaps he just didn't want to go alone.

He glanced up and smiled. Her smile back at him was pure reflex. 'Will they mind?' she asked.

'A local celebrity coming to their party! You must be joking. If I don't bring you they'll be disappointed.'

There was her answer. She was invited as a friend. He probably didn't like the idea of her sitting alone when there was no need. He was being kind.

'It's time I went to bed.' She glanced across at the fire.

'Don't worry about it,' he said, following the line of her gaze. 'I'm not going up for a while. I'll read for a bit and deal with the fire before I go up.'

'Is it a formal party?'

'Just a few friends. They'll be pleased to see you.'

He didn't add that it would please him for her to accept. He didn't say he wanted her company.

What did she expect? 'It'll be nice. Thank you.'

Another trip to Newport and Kate was satisfied. She'd found a pair of well-cut black trousers that would supplement her wardrobe back in London and a stunning evening top in a rich burgundy. For a girl who'd just given up a very well-paid job to go freelance it was a total extravagance—but irresistible.

Besides, how many dates with Gideon would she

have? Despite knowing it was nothing of the sort, she couldn't prevent a small part of her brain insisting that it was a *kind* of a date.

She smeared on the faintest trace of lipgloss over the dark burgundy lipstick, another unnecessary purchase to go with the black high-heeled stilettos she'd bought to go with the trousers.

What the heck? She had a lifetime to economise if she had to. Tonight she wasn't going to think about it.

Along the landing there were sounds of Gideon getting ready. Tilly and Jemima had gone to Emily's and the house was eerily quiet. She let herself out of the bedroom and went downstairs to wait.

'Ready?'

She turned and Gideon was standing at the top of the stairs. 'Is it time we left?'

There was something about Gideon tonight that reminded her of how he'd been all those years ago. The weariness she'd noticed about him had almost vanished. He seemed alive.

Or was that wishful thinking? Her heart had jammed up in her throat and she found it difficult to speak. No one who knew her in London would believe that was possible. Not Kate Simmonds, the voice of LA.

She reached up and checked the backs of her earrings were in place, not because she had to but because she needed to do something. And then, 'Oh, I bought some flowers. I left them in the utility room.'

Gideon walked past her and opened the door. He pulled the bouquet out of the bucket. 'These are beautiful.'

'Really? I wasn't sure what kind of colour scheme

they had but I thought yellow and cream goes with anything.'

He laid the bouquet on the granite surface of the central island and walked towards her. His hand reached out to push her hair away from her face; his fingers hovered about her cheek. 'Will you stop it? They'll be pleased to see you. You didn't have to bring anything.'

'No, but—'

'There are no buts, Kate.' His thumb gently caressed along her cheekbone and his eyes impaled her. 'Have I told you how beautiful you look?'

Kate Simmonds, former LA correspondent, ought to have had an answer, but the words stuck in her throat. She was so far out of her depth and going down for the third time.

He moved closer. His mouth was millimetres from hers. 'You are beautiful, Kate. You always have been.'

She laughed nervously. 'That's not true. You certainly didn't think so.'

Gideon stepped back, watching her. 'I wondered if you remembered,' he said simply. Then he took her by the hand and led her to the sofa.

She followed because she didn't know what else to do. Little shots of electricity were shooting up her arm and her head refused to process any information.

'I meant to tell you last night.' He broke off and turned away. Then he sat next to her and took hold of her hand. For a few moments he studied her palm, tracing the lines with his forefinger.

'I...' He stopped again and smiled. That half-smile that had her stomach flipping over. 'Kate, I...' He began again. Inside Kate a small flower was blossoming. A tiny flicker of confidence, something that had eluded her for such a long, long time. 'When you were seventeen, that first summer, when I came to the island…'

She nodded. His finger was moving against her palm and she didn't much care what he had to say. But she understood. She understood he understood. If that made any sense…

'I know. I followed you around like a lap-dog.'

His voice broke on a laugh. 'Did I hurt you?'

'No.' And then, 'A little. But Laura was lovely, she—'

'It didn't mean you weren't,' he cut in. 'You were seventeen. I was twenty-six. Nine years! It was a lifetime then.'

She nodded. She wanted to say *And now?* but didn't dare. In a way it was still a lifetime. He'd experienced so much. The birth of two children. The death of the wife he'd loved. In such a way.

'I did notice you.' He lifted her palm to his lips and kissed it. 'You were beautiful at seventeen but it would have been wrong, Kate.'

And now? The voice in her head was almost screaming the question. *Is it wrong now?*

'Sharing a house with you is sending me out of my mind.' He reached out and touched her hair.

Her heart was pounding so fast she could scarcely breathe. She didn't dare move in case he stopped— and she didn't want that. This was a moment she'd remember until the day she died.

Please God, don't let him stop.

'Kate?' His voice was questioning, his eyes searched her face for some kind of answer. And then he kissed her.

With every beat of her heart her soul was shouting out how much she loved him. Desperately. Fearfully.

This couldn't be happening. Fate would surely discover a way of robbing her of this happiness. It was too perfect to be trusted.

His kiss became more confident. More demanding. *Was this why she'd stayed on the island?* Was this what she'd been hoping for?

She felt as if she was standing on the brink, looking down. From here it was a choice. She could walk forwards or she could turn back.

And what choice was there? She loved him. She'd always loved him.

She let her right hand move up to push through his hair and cradle his head close. She felt his tongue flick against her lips and heard the soft murmur she gave.

If she died now, it would have been worth it.

His mouth was insistent against hers, dragging a response from her. Hungry. As though he'd been waiting for this for as long as she had.

'Kate…' His voice was ragged. He pulled back and his thumb caressed her swollen lips. He laid his forehead against hers while his breath steadied. 'If we carry on like this we aren't going to make the party.'

And did she care? 'I suppose not.'

He stood up in one swift movement. Kate followed. Gideon took hold of her hand, pausing to look down at their interlocked fingers. Then he walked towards the kitchen. 'Don't forget your flowers.'

Kate picked them off the worktop and made a show of smelling them. Hothoused and showy, they didn't have much scent, but Kate didn't notice. Every sense was filled up with Gideon, how his hand felt in hers, how fantastic he looked in his suede leather jacket, how the bristles on his chin still showed even though he'd shaved only half an hour before.

'Ready?'

She nodded.

He led her out on to the gravel drive. Her high heels scrunched against the tiny stones and she shivered in the night air.

This was unbelievable. Completely unbelievable. As though finally her fairy godmother had materialised. At last she'd waved her magic wand and all Kate's secret dreams were coming true.

They drove in his car, a high four-wheel drive Land Rover. Kate sat in a daze. It could have been a golden carriage conjured out of a pumpkin for all she knew.

The only thing that pierced her consciousness was that she was with Gideon—and he wanted to be there. For years she'd been on the edge, never quite being good enough.

And now? Now she had it all.

His leg moved as he changed gear and Kate knew how his muscles clenched and unclenched. His hands stroked the leather steering wheel and she felt it as if he was touching her skin.

She swallowed, trying to control the anticipation that was sitting in the pit of her stomach. 'Who will be there?'

He glanced across at her. 'Most of the old crowd. Debbie would have been, of course, but she's in hospital. Emily is taking care of most of the neighbourhood children. She's got her three, my two and Tom and Paula's two.'

'Brave woman.'

He smiled. 'We think so.'

Kate pleated the chiffon hem of her top. 'Did she mind not coming?'

'Not really. She's a little younger than us.' He smiled. 'Well, actually she's the same age as you.'

He slid the car into a parking space and came round to help her down. His fingers lightly grazed the sensitive skin on the inside of her forearm before linking with hers. It took all her control not to whimper.

She was so aware of him, the way he moved, turned his head, smiled, laughed. She could have written a PhD on him.

The small voice of reason kept whispering that this was stupid. That she'd be hurt. But it was easy to suppress. It was hard to walk away from something she'd always wanted. So much easier to pretend it would be perfect.

Together they walked towards the village hall. Its municipal appearance had been softened by small candles in a variety of lanterns.

Kate hesitated at the door.

'What is it?' Gideon asked, turning her to look at him.

From behind the door Kate could hear the sounds of laughter, conversation and music. *What would they think if she walked in with Gideon?*

She glanced down at their joined hands, then back at his incredible blue eyes. 'People will talk,' she said.

The corners of his eyes creased. 'Let them.'

He pushed open the door and led her into the hall. Kate's eyes took a moment to adjust to the comparative gloom. All she was aware of was a mass of people and the sudden hiatus in conversation as those near the door turned to look at them.

She was completely conscious of her hand lying in

Gideon's. Anxious about what other people would be thinking. Her other hand gripped the flowers she'd brought a little too tightly.

The bland setting of the hall had been transformed with paper streamers and yet more garden lanterns. At the far end there were trestle tables covered with paper tablecloths and laden with food.

Grey plastic chairs lined the walls and the music thumped out with far too much bass—but to Kate, her hand in Gideon's, it was perfect. More perfect than any of the first night parties or grand society events she'd covered as a reporter.

'You brought her!' Out of one group a woman in a forest-green shift dress stepped forward to greet them. She smiled at Kate and leant up to kiss Gideon on the cheek. 'I'm so glad you came.'

Gideon's arm moved to clamp about her waist as he said, 'Kate, this is Harriet Wootton. One half of the couple who beat us all up the aisle.'

Kate returned the smile and offered her the bouquet. 'Happy anniversary. I hope you don't mind my coming to your party.'

Harriet waved her words aside. 'These are just beautiful,' she said, pulling back the cream paper to look at the roses. 'I love flowers. I'll put them in some water in a minute, but first I must introduce you to some people. Everyone's dying to meet you.'

Kate glanced up at Gideon, who winked.

'How is Debbie getting on?' Harriet asked, leading them both towards the centre of the room.

'Bored.'

Harriet gave a gurgle of laughter. 'I spoke to her a couple of days ago and she was going up the wall then. Missing the boys, of course.'

Her gaze suddenly drifted away. Kate's followed in time to see a portly man standing on a chair trying to do something with paper lanterns.

'Gideon,' she said, turning to look at him. 'Go and sort out Andrew. He'll fall off that chair in a minute.'

Kate wanted to protest but knew she couldn't. It was ridiculous how vulnerable she felt when Gideon walked away. How could a woman who'd marched up to A list celebrities and forced a conversation on them be so pathetic now?

'Now, who do you know?' Harriet mused, searching the group nearest her.

Then a face Kate did remember detached herself from the crowd. Her long blonde hair had been cut short but other than that she hadn't changed at all.

'Katie!' she said, her arms outstretched. 'I don't believe it. How long have you been home?'

'Liz,' she said with relief.

Her old schoolfriend flung her arms round her. 'When did you come back? Why did no one tell me?'

'I came back for Aunt Babs's funeral,' Kate said, emerging from Liz's hug.

Her friend's face immediately shadowed. 'Of course, I forgot for a moment. I was so sorry to hear the news. And Debbie, how's she doing? Isn't she expecting her third?' Questions tumbled out of her mouth.

Kate filled her in and turned to find Harriet had disappeared. She located her by the door, talking with a couple who'd just arrived, still clutching the bouquet in her hand.

'It's so great to see you!' Liz exclaimed. 'Let's get a drink, something to eat and have a good gossip. I suggest you avoid the vol-au-vents because I brought those.' She pushed her way through a small huddle of people with a laughing smile. Kate followed in her wake.

Considering she had been to extraordinary lengths to avoid returning to the island, this felt strangely natural, Kate thought. There was a strong sense of home-coming. It was almost as though she'd never been away, picking up old threads, old friendships.

Piles of paper plates and plastic cups were on a nearby table, along with boxes of wine and cartons of fruit juice. Kate put her plastic wine glass beneath the wine box tap and waited while Liz did the same.

'It's strange to be back, isn't it?' Liz said. 'It seems like yesterday we came here for Paula's eighteenth. Do you remember?'

Kate remembered. Her eyes twinkled above the rim of her glass. She remembered how Christopher Matthews had tipped a bag of flour on Paula's head and the girls, all outraged, had taken her to wash it out. And that was when the fun had started.

Liz started to giggle. 'It turned to glue,' she said on a hiccup.

The years disappeared. Kate wiped at her eyes in an effort not to cry with laughter. She'd been wrong not to come back.

She should have come home. She'd thrown away so many good memories, so many fantastic friends, in place of what? Everything she hated most about her life had followed her wherever she went; the good things were here. With the people she loved.

Her eyes followed to where Gideon was standing amongst a group near the anniversary cake. He looked up at that moment and his eyes met hers.

He smiled. Intimate and inclusive. She couldn't remember the last time she'd been at a party and felt anything other than incredibly alone.

Then a woman she didn't recognise spoke to him and he bent to hear what she'd said. The connection between them was broken.

'Look!' Liz said, pulling her to a nearby table. 'Photographs.'

She sat down and opened the large padded white album. Kate took the chair next to her, watching as Liz flicked through the portrait photographs.

'Didn't Harriet look lovely? She was so thin. And Andrew wasn't bald then,' Liz remarked, turning the pages quickly. 'This is the one I wanted.' She stopped at a photograph of family and friends. 'There's your Debbie.'

Kate looked where she was pointing. Debbie, ten years younger, was standing next to an equally youthful-looking Mike.

'I remember that dress,' Kate remarked. 'I was with her when she bought it. We thought it was the epitome of good taste.'

Liz smiled, scanning all the familiar faces.

'There's Laura and Gideon.'

Kate's gaze had reached them in the line-up at precisely the same moment. Gideon was laughing, his face turned towards Laura, who was standing clutching her bridesmaid's bouquet.

Just as she remembered him. Sunshine and laughter. Before tragedy had swiped at his life.

'There'll be a better one of Laura,' Liz said, flicking backwards. 'I must have gone past it. Laura was Harriet's bridesmaid. Here.'

Laura Bannerman in a pale shade of apricot. Her ice-blonde hair curled and pulled up at the sides on flower-covered combs. Beside her the other two bridesmaids looked short and dumpy. Even the bride was slightly overshadowed.

Laura had been the embodiment of a dream. Probably the most beautiful woman Kate had ever seen close up—and that was saying something. She could have been a model. She had been tall and willowy, with perfect skin and the kind of bone structure that would have made her lovely even at eighty.

'You heard about her suicide, I suppose?' Liz was saying.

'Only recently. I was in LA at the time and missed hearing it somehow. Perhaps Debbie thought Babs had told me and vice versa.'

'It was awful. She swallowed a bottle of paracetamol. I didn't know something so simple could be so dangerous. Left Gideon with two little girls to bring up by himself.'

Kate swallowed, forcing her voice to sound natural. 'I know. I'm helping out while Debs is in hospital. She was collecting his girls from school and Nursery while he's between nannies.'

'Oh.' Liz stood and picked up her plastic glass. 'I haven't seen him in months. How's he doing now?'

Kate's eyes travelled the room and found him a few feet away from where he'd been last time. Rachel Boyle was standing at his elbow, clutching a paper plate in her hand.

She picked up her own glass. 'Missing Laura. Probably always will.'

How could he ever move on from such a tragedy? *Second best.* The words popped into her head. What was it Debbie had said? Something about Gideon never marrying again because it could only be second best?

Beside her, Liz snorted. 'I know this isn't the PC thing to say, but...' She sipped her wine. 'I think his life is probably a lot easier now.'

Kate looked across at her, surprised.

'Well, she was always highly strung, wasn't she?' she said apologetically. 'And, if you think about it, she was always inclined to be depressed. And she made a real fuss about being pregnant. Couldn't cope with losing her figure.'

Laura? Kate had never heard her spoken of in anything but reverential tones. Almost sanctified in her perfection.

'I know it's not her fault,' Liz went on. 'And I do think it's awful she killed herself...but don't you think she must have been a real pain to live with? I couldn't *manage* it for a couple of weeks let alone the years Gideon stayed with it.'

Kate felt as if her feet had been cemented to the floor. She heard Liz say something about getting a chicken leg before they all disappeared but she made an excuse.

Maybe she wasn't second best? Maybe, just maybe...

She started to walk back into the centre of the room. Couples had begun to take to the floor. She weaved through them, looking for Gideon. Was it really possible his life hadn't been as perfect as she supposed?

She had never thought about what it must have been like living with someone so desperately unhappy. So unhappy she'd thought it worth ending her life for.

Laura Bannerman hadn't had it all at all. In many, many ways Kate had more. It was a blinding revelation.

Day after day, month after month of someone else's misery and hurt must grind you down. And how much worse when that someone was a person you loved?

Then she saw him. Taller than the men he stood with, far, far better looking. With Laura he'd been one half of a golden couple. Perhaps their day-to-day life had been different?

Was nothing as it seemed?

He looked up and mouthed at her to stay still. Then he detached himself from the crowd and made his way across the hall towards her. 'Okay?' he asked. 'I lost you somewhere in the throng.'

'I met Liz Rutherford, except she isn't Rutherford any more. She's Winley now. She was my best friend at school.'

'I remember.'

Kate looked up, startled.

He smiled. 'She was the long-haired blonde one who used to sit on the wall with you and wait for me to finish work.'

She felt the flush spread up her neck and across her face. Once it had achieved total coverage it started to work on the intensity of colour.

Gideon reached out and stroked her burning cheek. 'Would you do it now?'

'Sit on the wall and wait for you?' she managed to ask. 'No. I don't think I would.'

His eyes widened at an answer he hadn't expected.

She smiled innocently up at him. 'The wall was awfully sharp in places. These days I think I'd just give you my number and see if you phoned.'

He gave a crack of laughter. 'I'd phone,' he said softly. Then he bent close to say, 'Dance with me?'

The floor disappeared from under her feet. 'I'd like that.'

Gideon's arm slipped about her waist and he pulled her in towards him. His eyes were on her face. Kate felt as if she'd stepped into a movie. Gradually everything around them became blurred and the only thing that remained in focus was them.

The soft suede of his jacket felt smooth beneath her fingers and his hand was warm on her waist. So many sensations. So much to remember.

She let her head relax on his chest and listened to the solid thud of his heart. The music swirled around her and she let her body move where he guided her.

Gideon Manser.

The world was shifting about and she didn't know what to make of it. Everything she'd thought was fixed and unalterable was changing.

Maybe the fact that Gideon already had children would mean he wouldn't mind her infertility. Maybe? Just maybe…

And then the tempo changed. Reluctantly Kate stepped back. For a moment Gideon looked at her as though he might pull her back into his arms and then he released her hand.

He glanced down at his watch. 'I've had enough of this. Shall we go home?'

Kate didn't need to check her watch to know they'd only been there little over an hour and a half. The evening had only just begun. The cake hadn't been cut.

She looked up into his eyes and saw the passion in

them. She didn't need to ask why he wanted to go home. It was blazoned in his face.

The question was, what did she want? Since Richard had left she'd been running scared. No relationships. She'd let no one near, but Gideon had crawled underneath her defences.

She drew a sharp intake of breath. He hadn't got under her defences. He'd always been inside them. Gideon was the other half of her. The man she was destined to love.

There was no decision to make. 'Let's go.'

CHAPTER NINE

GIDEON didn't say anything. He didn't show surprise or delight, he merely reached out to hold her hand. With a purposeful stride he threaded their way through the crowded village hall and out into the car park.

The night air bit through the thin fabric of her evening top and Kate shivered. His arms wrapped round her. 'Cold?'

Cold? Nervous? Kate wasn't sure what was making her shake the most.

'Here.' He shrugged out of his jacket and rested it across her shoulders.

'No,' she protested. 'You'll get cold.'

He just laughed, a carefree sound. 'I don't think so.'

Kate held the lapels of his jacket around her. It was still warm from his body. The faint scent of his aftershave hung about the fabric.

She loved him.

The drive back to the house was largely silent. Gideon seemed intent on the road and Kate's mind was incapable of thinking anything much. Her stomach had started to churn as though a million tiny butterflies had been let loose inside her.

Gideon swung round into the cottage drive and stopped the engine. The silence was deafening.

He turned to look at her. 'Home.'

Just one word but it meant so much to Kate. *Home.*

She'd always wanted that, and finally, with Gideon, she really felt as if she'd found it.

He opened the door and came round to help her out. She let him take her hand and stood still while he locked the doors. Then they turned towards the cottage.

Neither said anything. There was no need for words. The front door shut with a reverberating bang, loud in the quiet of the country air.

Kate stood wide-eyed, waiting. Not a virgin but as nervous as she'd been that first time. And Gideon? What was he feeling?

He slid his hands inside his jacket, still resting around her shoulders. With infinite slowness he pushed it aside until it fell to the floor. Kate shivered with anticipation, her eyes on his face.

She wanted to tell him how much she loved him but the words wouldn't come out. And then the moment for talking passed. She was in his arms, his strong hands pulling her pliant body in close to his, his tongue teasing her lips.

'You're so beautiful,' he murmured against her mouth, and Kate wanted to laugh with the sheer joy of the moment.

Gideon thought she was beautiful.

He pulled away and his hand stroked the side of her face. Then he smiled. The smile she remembered from all those years ago. The smile she treasured somewhere deep with her. 'Let's go to bed?'

Her answer was a kiss. This was the moment she'd been waiting for, perhaps since that first summer. Every sense was fully occupied; there was no room for any considerations of past or future. There was only now. This one moment in time.

And this moment was perfect.

He led her up the narrow staircase and pulled her towards his bedroom at the end of the landing. An antique brass bedstead dominated the room. Either side were marble-topped tables with matching table lamps.

Gideon bent down to switch on the one nearest to them. Its gentle light softened the darkness. And then he moved towards her, his strong hands pulling her towards him.

'Kate, do we need to use any protection?'

She reached up and pressed a kiss against the side of his neck. 'No.'

Her conscience whispered that she ought to tell him why. She knew her single-word answer implied she was on the pill, but she couldn't bear the thought of spoiling this moment.

Not now. Not tonight. Not this first time, the inner voice pleaded.

And then the opportunity was gone. He was kissing her and she forgot everything but the way his hands moved across her body.

Gideon opened his eyes as the morning sunlight streamed through his bedroom window. And then he remembered.

Kate was so beautiful. And she was in his bed. He rolled over and let his eyes devour her. For so many years now he'd not let himself believe he would ever feel this level of contentment. A feeling of complete peace, as though his life had shifted into kilter and everything was in harmony once more.

And all because of Kate. The miracle healing Babs

had talked about had become reality. He looked down at her sleeping and realised how much he loved her.

She lay on her stomach, her arm flung out beside her in total abandonment, her smooth hair ruffled and dark against the white bedlinen.

Gideon leant over and pressed a kiss in the centre of her spine and smiled at the small murmur of appreciation that came from deep within her throat. Then he slid his hand down the full length of her back, loving the feeling of her smooth skin.

If he told her he loved her, how would she react? Kate had promised to stay until Debbie's baby was born. No longer. Would last night make any difference to her plans?

He didn't hope it. He'd always known their lives were incompatible. He was tied to this place as securely as if he were shackled and she...

She was driven to succeed. Beautiful, clever, ambitious and talented. He could go on and on. So many reasons why she wouldn't stay. There was just one why she would.

Because she loved him.

And why would she love him? Why would someone like Kate settle for the life he had to offer her?

He let his palm slide across her shoulder blades, trying to convey his love for her in the tenderness of his touch. As his eyes followed the path of his fingers he noticed a small, neat scar. A perfect circle.

Like a burn.

A small, circle-like burn. His fingers moved across the tell-tale mark on her back.

He felt her tense and then she rolled over to look up at him. His mouth formed the shape of a question, but he didn't have to ask it.

'It's a burn,' she stated bluntly. 'From a cigarette. I know, it's very ugly.'

'Ugly?' His hands smoothed her shiny hair back from her face. 'What are you talking about?'

She didn't look away from him but he sensed her desperation to do so. A need to hide from him. And then she said slowly, 'My stepfather did it. Once when he was angry. My mother had drunk too much and was asleep on the sitting room floor. She'd used the rent money. And...'

She couldn't carry on; her voice was lost in the tears she was fighting back.

Gideon leant forward and softly kissed her. 'Thank God he put you in care.'

He saw the arrested look in her eyes and then the slow smile. 'Yes.'

'You're beautiful. Inside and out.'

And then her smile blossomed, her eyes lost the hurt and vulnerable look she so often carried with her. Her hands wound round his neck and pulled him in close for a deep and sweetly intoxicating kiss.

He felt his gut tighten and he pulled her long, warm body against his. As he wrapped his arms about her he felt an overwhelming sense of rightness. Of possessiveness. She belonged with him.

Gideon kissed her hair and then with trembling hands pushed the silky softness aside. He would make her believe that. He would love her until the day he died and he would keep her safe.

Her hands swept up the sides of his body and fastened his mouth on hers.

When they woke again it was past ten o'clock. As Kate forced herself into consciousness she became aware of the imperative shrill summons of a telephone.

'Gideon?'

He prised open his eyes and took a moment for them to focus.

'It's the phone,' she prompted, a smile playing about her mouth. She'd never imagined she'd know what he looked like first thing in the morning. The shadow of dark hair on his chin and sleep-heavy eyes, still unbelievably sexy.

'It'll be Emily. I said I'd pick up the girls at eleven. Have we overslept?' he asked, sitting up and pulling a hand across his face.

Then he swung his legs out of the bed and stood up. Kate leant up on one elbow and resisted the urge to wolf whistle.

He turned and caught something of the glint in her eye because he said, 'Behave,' as he leant over to give her a kiss.

Then he pulled on the trousers he'd discarded on the floor the night before and went to answer the telephone.

Kate couldn't hear what he was saying. His voice was an incomprehensible mumble. She lay back on the feather pillows and stared at the ceiling.

Everything had changed. The unbelievable had happened. She loved him and he...

She let her eyes roam around the room.

He what?

Loved her?

Just because she wanted him to love her didn't make it reality. Last night it hadn't felt as if they needed to talk but perhaps that had been a mistake.

They'd begun a physical relationship without establishing any of the ground rules. There was so much she didn't know about him. About what he wanted.

And there was so much he didn't know about her. *Her infertility.* Kate sat up and hugged the pillow into her. She hadn't been fair to start a physical relationship with him when she hadn't told him something that had really started to define her life. However much she'd like to believe it wouldn't matter to him, it wasn't right not to have told him.

Perhaps he didn't want any more children? After his experience it was quite possible he didn't. If so, it wouldn't matter to him.

But he'd said he and Laura had wanted more children. So perhaps it would matter.

Kate chewed on her bottom lip. Or maybe he didn't feel that way about her at all. She was imagining happy ever after and he might be thinking in terms of a short respite.

He'd only said she was beautiful. It didn't really amount to a declaration of undying passion.

And Laura had been beautiful too. More beautiful than she was. Kate looked over to the side of the bed where Gideon had slept. Her eyes immediately lighted on what she'd been looking for.

Laura.

Laura in the mahogany frame. Forever young. Forever beautiful.

And this had been Laura's home. Laura's bedroom. Laura's bed?

And Gideon had been Laura's husband.

Was she only second best? There because Laura wasn't?

Kate pushed back the duvet and searched about the room for her discarded clothes. She found her underwear on the floor at the foot of the bed, her trousers and evening top by the door.

They would have to talk—but she could only do that with her clothes on. She was going to need every ounce of confidence. *What if he was already regretting what he'd done?*

The desperate uncertainty swirled about her. He hadn't looked as if he minded waking up to find her in his bed. But then he'd hardly been awake.

She pulled the door of his bedroom open and listened. Gideon was no longer on the telephone and she heard sounds coming from the kitchen. She needed to get dressed.

Pausing only to pick up her shoes, she scurried along the landing to what had become her room. Once inside, she shut the door and stood for a moment with her back resting against it. *What had she done?*

After Richard she'd promised herself she would never allow herself to be so vulnerable again. But last night she'd stepped off the cliff and fallen in the sea. Now she was floundering about. Desperately scared of being hurt. Too frightened to believe Gideon would ever come to care for her.

Being rejected by Richard had made her feel as if steel had entered her soul. Being rejected by Gideon would be like having her soul sucked out. There was no comparison. She'd be like the living dead.

When she'd met Richard she'd been in love with the idea of love. She'd wanted to belong. But Gideon...

Gideon was the other half of who she wanted to be. He was the man she wanted to walk through the rest of her life with. She wanted to be there for him through all the good and the bad times.

But what did he want?

She quickly threw her clothes on the bed and went to the drawer to pull out her linen trousers and brown jumper. Taking clean underwear with her, she hurried through to the *en suite* bathroom.

The water was fresh and cool but Kate didn't dare waste a moment. By the time Gideon returned upstairs she wanted to be dressed, prepared and ready to face whatever he said next.

As she pulled her jumper over her head she heard the door to her room open.

'Kate?'

She grabbed a towel and rubbed at her hair as she walked back through into the bedroom. She hardly dared look at him. Just one glance at his face and she'd know.

'Was it Emily?' she asked.

He stood in the doorway, a mug of tea in his hand. And his eyes were…confused—which told her nothing.

'It was Mike.'

She dropped the towel. 'Mike!' A thousand possibilities whizzed through her mind before Gideon could continue.

'Debbie's had the baby. It's a girl. Five pounds, twelve ounces. Mother and baby are doing fine.'

Kate sat down on the bed. 'Thank God. And Debbie's really fine?'

He came into the room and handed her the mug. 'You can judge for yourself. She'd like to see you. As soon as you can possibly make it after two, which is when normal visiting hours start.'

As the immediate relief passed, reality began to sink in. She was going to see Debbie in hospital—

with her tiny newborn baby. Kate wrapped her hands around the warmth of her mug.

She knew it would hurt. Kate could imagine the feeling without any difficulty. However much she loved Debbie it would still send pangs of anguish leaping through her. But she would do it.

And she felt proud of that.

'Do you want to drink that downstairs?' Gideon asked, nodding towards her tea. 'I thought you'd still be in bed.'

'I took the chance to grab a shower.' She glanced up at him.

For so long her life had been defined by her inability to have children. She would have thought the prospect of seeing Debbie's baby would drive everything else from her mind—but now she had a deeper concern.

Her future happiness depended on Gideon. On how he reacted to her news.

And whether he thought he could ever love her.

He held out his hand and she took it. He pulled her to her feet. 'I rang Emily and she'll keep the girls for me. Tom's already driven over to collect his two, so she's happy to hang on to mine until later.'

His arms came round her waist. 'I could come with you to see Debbie. We could drive over to Newport, get some lunch, try and find something for the baby. Some flowers for Debbie. What do you think?'

Kate let her fingers rest on his bare chest. His skin was tanned from the summer, warm to the touch. She wanted to ask him how he felt about her but something held her silent.

Richard had always said she planned too much, tried to control everything. This time she'd be different. She'd accept what Gideon had to offer. She'd take each precious day as it came.

'Is there much open in Newport on a Sunday?'

He smiled, the laughter back in his blue eyes. 'To be honest, I've not got the faintest idea. Let's go and see.'

Time with Gideon. Just the two of them. More time to convince him that she could make him happy—if only he gave them a chance. Not second best, but a new beginning.

She just needed more time.

The uncertainty was poignantly painful—but had to be worth the risk. Didn't it?

More time with Gideon would mean she'd come to love him more. It was inevitable. The more she knew him, the more she admired and trusted him.

The more she loved him.

She reached up to kiss him. 'Lunch would be great.'

If the right moment arose she would tell him about her infertility. It wasn't the kind of thing you could just throw into the conversation—but she would tell him. Today. Before they saw Debbie's baby. That would be best.

'Bring your tea downstairs and I'll fix us breakfast.'

It was a risk. But she'd do it.

Two o'clock came sooner than Kate could have believed possible. She glanced across at Gideon as he parked the Land Rover in the hospital car park.

She hadn't told him. Somehow that perfect moment had never come. And now it was too late to do it before she saw Debbie's baby.

Her stomach was churning with a nervous mix of

fear and anticipation. And sorrow. Everything was tempered with that. The knowledge she would never have a child of her own still burned within her. But there was triumph too.

She was doing the unthinkable. She was facing her greatest sadness head on. It was something to be proud of.

The hospital had that distinctive smell that always reminded her of her own stay there. She clutched the small pink teddy bear they'd bought and Gideon held the bouquet of pink and white flowers.

Her heart was pounding and seemed to have swollen to triple its normal size. But Gideon was there. Strong. Supportive. If he hadn't been there she might well have turned back in the car park. Run away while she still had the chance.

Her shoes clicked along the corridors as they came closer to the ward where Debbie was. A formidable nurse with an unusually large quantity of facial hair sat at the desk and directed them towards an end room.

Kate just let it happen. If Gideon wondered why she'd suddenly become so silent he didn't say anything.

The bed by the window was empty, curtains had been drawn around the second, but in the third she located Debbie. Kate hesitated by the door. Uncertain whether she could make it further into the room.

And then she had no choice as Debbie looked up and smiled. 'Kate. You came.'

'Of course I came. I told you I would.' She walked forward and hovered by the end of the bed. 'We—' she gestured back at Gideon who'd hung behind '—

brought you this. Well, not you, exactly. This is for the baby.'

She held out the small teddy bear with its bright pink bow. 'We added the bow,' she said awkwardly. 'We bought that in the card shop.'

'It's lovely.'

Kate stood, feeling awkward, taking in Debbie's slightly blotchy face and the plastic name tag round her wrist. Her eyes kept drifting to the transparent cot to the right of the bed but she didn't move closer.

Debbie leant over to put the teddy at the end of the crib. Then she turned and smiled, a stunning contrast from Kate's earlier visits when Debbie had been bored, crotchety and desperate to get home.

Gideon stepped forward and handed her the bouquet with a kiss on her cheek. 'Congratulations. Was the waiting worth it?' he asked with a smile.

'At least I know the type of baby I've got! Determined from the beginning,' Debbie answered. The pride in her voice made Kate hurt. She would never know what this felt like. Never. She'd never have that sense of pride and achievement.

She'd only been fooling herself to imagine she could do this. Not even Gideon's presence was going to make this possible.

She almost ran then. But Debbie looked at her and patted the side of the bed. 'Would you like to meet her?' She glanced over at the plastic cot on wheels 'She's about to wake for a feed.'

Then Kate heard faint snuffling sounds. Almost a whimper. It screwed her heart up as easily as if it had been a tissue.

'Gideon, will you pass her to me?'

Kate watched with a fatalistic fascination as he

walked over to the sterile crib. It probably only took a few seconds but to Kate it felt like an eternity, like one of those sporting replay clips.

Then Gideon reached down and lifted out a tiny bundle of white Babygro. Experienced hands, Kate thought, watching him cradle the baby close to his chest.

She was so tiny. So newborn. Her little feet rested frog-like against the grey of his jumper.

'Do you want her now?' he asked, his eyes on Debbie.

Kate watched, mesmerized, as the baby snuffled some more. Her face was scrunched up and her fist was rammed in her mouth.

'I'll feed her. Hopefully she'll then be in a good mood to meet you both properly.'

Gideon handed the baby over to Debbie.

'Do you want me to put the flowers in a vase?' he asked.

Debbie stroked her daughter's cheek with one forefinger and then looked up. 'Thank you. If you ask the nurse on duty where the vases are, she'll be able to show you.'

'I know where they're kept.'

His shoes squeaked on the floor. Kate watched him go. *Of course he knew where the vases were kept.* Why hadn't she thought of that before?

Gideon had been here before. Twice before. When his own children had been born. Perhaps Laura had even been in this room. Was it a good memory or a bad memory?

Debbie lowered the cup of her feeding bra and latched her baby girl on. 'She's a really good feeder. The baby over there—' she nodded to the area behind the curtain '—is a real pain. I think he wants to open his mouth and have the milk dropped in!'

She stopped and studied Kate's face. 'I'm sorry. I wasn't thinking.' She half smiled. 'I'm always so smug after I've given birth. You wouldn't think any other woman had ever done it before. Are you all right?'

Kate stared at the way Debbie's fingers splayed out around the tiny head, saw the impossibly small hand spread out on her mother's breast and listened to the small contented sounds coming from the infant.

She looked up and found Debbie watching her. She didn't want her to say anything more, didn't want her to thank her for coming. She certainly didn't want her sympathy. She couldn't bear that. Her control was hanging by a thread.

'Have you given her a name yet?' she asked quickly.

Debbie looked past her shoulder to the door. 'Did you find a vase?'

'Choice of two,' Gideon replied, coming back into the room. 'I settled on this one.' He set a plain silver vase on the melamine table and started to unwrap the paper round the flowers. 'This isn't going to be the most artistic arrangement.'

'Where are the girls?' Debbie asked, inserting her little finger into the baby's mouth to detach her from her nipple.

Kate watched, fascinated. The pain sat like a stone in her chest but she couldn't resist watching every detail.

'With Emily. Mike phoned with the news and I couldn't miss being one of the first to meet this little lady.' He walked round to the visitors' chair and moved some magazines aside before sitting down.

Debbie dextrously transferred the baby to the other breast. 'Of course, I forgot! It was Harriet's anniversary party. How did it go?'

'I think it went well. Everyone seemed to be having a good time. What do you think, Kate?'

Kate mumbled something positive. At least she hoped it sounded positive. Her relationship with Gideon was still such a recent development she wasn't sure she wanted anyone knowing about it yet, not even Debbie.

'Oh, did you go too?' Debbie asked, looking directly at Kate. There was a small beat before her eyes flicked across to Gideon, then back to Kate.

Without a doubt she was adding two and two and coming up with the right answer. Kate looked down at her knees. Debbie had known how she'd felt about Gideon all those years ago. She would be itching to interrogate her at the first possible opportunity. *And what would she say?*

Then the feed was finished. Debbie lifted her daughter upright and held her tiny face between her thumb and forefinger, supporting her chin and sitting her upright. Her other hand moved in small, firm circles on her back.

'Would you like to hold her?'

Kate jumped and turned back to look at Debbie. She was watching her closely, trying to gauge her reaction. 'I...I don't...I mean, I think I ought...'

'She won't break, Kate,' Debbie insisted.

Kate kept her eyes on Debbie's face. 'I've never held a baby,' she whispered. 'She's so tiny.'

'Use a pillow for support if you're worried.' She turned and pulled one out from the pile behind her.

Kate's heart was hammering against her chest, far too large for the cavity it inhabited. She set the pillow across her knee.

'Gideon, will you hand her to Kate?' Debbie held out her daughter to him.

Vaguely it occurred to Kate that he must be thinking she was ridiculous, but she couldn't help it. If only she'd told him about her infertility.

She glanced up at him as he walked across to her but then her attention was taken up with being given this tiny little being.

Kate held out her arm in the way she'd seen Debbie do and accepted the tiny bundle. *Warm.* The baby was warm. Another human being. It really was a miracle. Debbie's bump had become a little life.

'So, does she have a name yet?' Kate asked, aware that she was holding the baby stiffly and wishing she could just relax into it.

'Mike and I were talking about it this morning. We didn't expect a girl. Not after two boys, somehow. But we thought Mary. It's Mike's mother's name and my mum's middle one.'

Mary. It suited her. Kate looked down, amazed at the way her tiny mouth was constantly moving.

'So we thought we'd combine that with Katherine. Katherine Mary.'

Kate looked up.

'After you. Do you mind a new little Katie?'

Did she mind? No, she didn't mind. She felt the hot tears start to well up behind her eyes but didn't have a hand to deal with them.

'Of course I don't mind,' she managed, her voice choked.

Little Katie.

Her tiny chest was heaving up and down, her arms were relaxed and her whole body satiated from her feed. There was such potential in this tiny person. A whole lifetime ahead of her.

She'd two parents to love and care for her and Kate felt a sudden, surprising, protectiveness towards her.

Gideon moved. He came and sat next to her and she could feel his arm behind her back, his head close to hers.

'I think Katie is a great name,' he said, reaching out to touch the soft skin of little Katie's face.

'Would you like to hold her?' Debbie asked Gideon.

'No, Kate's—'

'Had enough,' Kate cut in.

She was aware of his quick glance at her and then he dextrously reached round to pick little Katie up. 'Hello, gorgeous,' he said.

Little Katie seemed oblivious. Her eyes were screwed tightly shut.

Kate stood up and smoothed out her linen trousers and then gave Debbie back her pillow. 'Thank you,' she whispered, placing a soft kiss on Debbie's cheek. 'She's a darling.'

Debbie smiled and squeezed her hand. Two small gestures which conveyed everything to Kate. There was no need of words, no long explanations. Debbie knew all there was to know. And Kate knew she knew.

She went to sit in the chair Gideon had vacated.

He was standing at the end of the bed, little Katie tucked in the crook of his arm.

It made Kate's heart contract painfully and then it seemed to jump up into her throat, making it difficult to swallow.

Gideon had been here and done this before. He'd held his own children when they'd been born. He made it all look so natural—and that was because, for him, it was. It was part of his experience.

And the mother of his children was Laura. The Laura who'd painted the magical bedroom for Jemima. The Laura who'd helped him set up the Quay Inn from its inception.

Laura, whom she remembered from when they'd first started dating. She remembered the way Gideon had looked at her. The love in his face, the laughter.

Which would make her second best. Again.

At seventeen she'd longed to be Laura. Had wondered what it would be like to live in the beautiful big house high on the cliffs. She'd wanted to know what it would be like to be everybody's darling.

But above everything she'd envied her Gideon. With a toss of her long blonde hair she'd drawn him towards her like a magnet. He hadn't looked right or left but had gone to her.

A golden couple. Inevitable. *Fated.*

And Kate had sat on the sidelines and watched. Loving him too—but not noticed. Too young, maybe, but her feelings had been real.

She knew that now. Just as Gideon had been destined to love Laura, she'd been destined to love him. She'd known the first time she'd seen him.

It had been different for him. He hadn't noticed her. He'd chosen Laura Bannerman. They'd married and bought a stunning house. Had extended and decorated it. Had planned for a long, long future there. Had built up a successful hotel and restaurant business. Had two children together...

The thoughts streamed through her head in a seamless flow. And she would be his second best.

Living another woman's life—simply because that woman was no longer alive to live it. Not chosen by him but *settled for* because he couldn't have 'perfect' any more. She didn't want to be the woman Gideon *settled for*. She couldn't live with the knowledge that he didn't love her.

Kate watched as Gideon carried the baby across to the transparent crib, which was tilted up at an angle.

'Do you want me to lie her down?' he asked Debbie.

Debbie nodded and reached out for a glass of water. Kate stood and poured her a glass. She was going through the motions but something inside had died.

She was going back to London.

This couldn't be her life. She couldn't step into Laura's shoes and live the life she should have had. There had to be something that was hers. Hers and Gideon's.

And she knew she could never give him a child. She could never hope to replace Laura. She wouldn't be enough.

CHAPTER TEN

'YOU'RE looking tired, Debbie,' Gideon said. 'Little Katie will sleep for a while; you ought to do the same.'

She nodded and held her hand out to Kate. 'Will you come again?'

Kate drew a deep breath, uncertain what to say. 'I'll try and look in on you before I leave,' she said hesitantly. 'Now Katie's born safely I ought to be getting back home.'

'At least come in tomorrow,' Debbie protested.

'I'll see what the availability on the ferry is.' Kate leant forward and kissed Debbie's cheek. 'Get some sleep. I'll speak to you soon.'

She didn't look to see what effect her words had had on Gideon. Just a few hours earlier she'd been building castles in the sky, imagining a future with him.

It was all make-believe. In the cold light of day she knew it was fantasy, and the sooner she went back to reality the better.

She went to pick her black coat off the end of the bed, then she steeled herself to meet his eyes. 'Ready?'

A nerve pulsed in his neck. 'Let's go.'

He paused to say goodbye and then he followed her out of the room. She could hear his feet on the hard floor behind. She didn't turn round, didn't want to slow down for him to catch her up.

Then his hand reached out to stop her. 'Hang on a minute.' Kate came to an abrupt stop. His blue eyes were blazingly angry but his voice was tightly controlled. 'You're leaving? Just like that?'

She didn't need to ask whether he meant the hospital or the island. She knew. And he had every right to be angry.

Kate did up the buttons on her coat and feigned nonchalance. 'It was always the plan. After the baby arrived.'

She saw the hurt in his eyes, the questions he wanted to ask. Perhaps he would have asked them, but an orderly started down the corridor with a woman in a wheelchair and Kate knew she had a reprieve.

She needed to marshal her defences, work out in her head what it was she wanted to say. The truth wasn't an option.

For years she'd struggled with other people's pity. The feeling of not being quite good enough—and she knew she couldn't articulate that feeling to Gideon.

Besides, what could he say? She could cope with anything but his sympathy. She didn't want him to know about how empty and second best her infertility made her feel.

She didn't want him to know how much she loved him if he couldn't return it. He'd never said he loved her. However many reasons she could find for staying, it always came back to that.

It had taken seeing him with a baby in his arms to make her fully realise how right Debbie had been when she'd said Laura was an impossible act to follow. She should have listened.

Gideon released her arm and they turned towards

the exit. He didn't speak again until they were in the car. He put the key into the ignition and turned to look at her. 'I don't get it, Kate. Why the rush?'

'I've got a career to sort. This was only ever going to be a short respite. You knew that.' Kate reached into her pocket for a packet of mints. 'Originally I was going back the day after the funeral. Do you want one?' she asked, offering him the packet.

He stared down at it as though it were something strange. 'No. Thank you.' And then. 'What about us?'

Kate took out a mint. 'It was lovely but it was probably a mistake.' She watched a flicker of emotion pass over his face.

If he said he loved her now she'd stay. Kate knew it. If he told her he loved her it wouldn't matter that she'd never be as good as Laura. Second best. If he just said he loved her...

He turned away and switched on the engine. 'It's a sudden finish. What about the girls?'

Kate knew what it must feel like to die. Excruciating agony ripped through her. 'Emily's back now. You said she'd help. If you need me I can manage a few more days...'

'You've done enough.'

For one desperate moment she wanted to turn the clock back, to play the last twenty minutes completely differently. But then she glanced across at his profile and realised she was right. She'd loved him for such a long time; she wasn't strong enough for an affair with Gideon.

Last night had changed the rules and altered their relationship for all time. She wasn't strong enough to carry on as normal, knowing she was only a temporary fixture in his life. There only because his Laura wasn't.

They drove up the narrow lane and turned into the cottage driveway. He stopped the engine. 'I'd better collect the girls.'

Kate was already fiddling with the door handle. 'Yes, of course.'

'I'll check with Emily when I pick the girls up and see whether she can help me.'

Jemima and Tilly weren't her responsibility, she reminded herself. She wasn't to feel guilty. He'd managed perfectly well without her help before; he'd do so again. 'Right.' Then she climbed out and shut the door.

Gideon wasted no time in driving away, leaving Kate to let herself into the house alone. She dropped her handbag in the hall and went straight upstairs.

It felt as if she was ripping herself away from this place. She'd only lived here for two short weeks and yet it felt as if it was in her bones.

And that was why she had to leave. It wasn't healthy. For her. For Gideon. Or his girls. She would be living another woman's life.

Kate had no way of knowing what things in the house had been chosen by Laura. But Gideon would know. Every day of his life he would remember.

She sat on the edge of the bed and wrapped her arms round her waist, fighting back the tears. She couldn't let herself cry. She didn't do that. Ever. She was stronger than that.

Gideon wrenched the handbrake into place.

Kate was inside his house, probably packing. He didn't think he could cope with seeing it.

Behind him Jemima was talking, her voice high-pitched and excited. He glanced in his rearview mirror at her happy face and felt guilty. He hadn't heard one word in five she'd said. He'd just grunted in the odd place and it had seemed to satisfy her.

She was so pleased to see him and all he wanted to do was drive off into the distance. Anything to avoid seeing Kate getting ready to leave him.

He'd thought he'd experienced every negative emotion known to man—but he'd been wrong. He'd never known rejection like this. Kate was leaving him because she wanted to. She was going back to her life in London because that was where she wanted to be.

It was hard to deal with. His hands gripped the steering wheel. Actually, it was impossible to deal with. How could everything have changed so quickly? How could she walk away, seemingly without a backward glance?

Another look in the rearview mirror and he realised Jemima was waiting for an answer. 'What was that?' he asked.

'Is Kate home?'

'Yes.' *For now.* He should tell her Kate was planning on leaving, that Emily would be collecting her from school tomorrow, but he couldn't bring himself to do it.

He couldn't talk to Jemima about it while his own emotions were so churned up. If he could follow Kate to London he would do it. Anything to be with her.

But he couldn't leave the island—and she wouldn't stay.

His life was a mess. He had responsibility for two young lives and he was doing his best, but sometimes it all weighed so heavily.

He climbed out of the car and walked round to where Tilly sat in her car seat, her head tilted to one side as she slept. So like Laura.

Sometimes he missed her like a physical pain. But two years of missing had dulled the edge, softened the pain, just as Babs had said it would. He hadn't realised that until Kate had arrived on the island.

In two weeks his life had been transformed. Everything he'd taken as set in stone had altered. He'd vowed never to risk loving anyone again. The cost was too great.

Then Kate had come home. He'd known from the start that she would never stay on the island. At eighteen she'd been desperate to leave, anxious to try her wings in the wider world.

Now she was successful beyond her wildest dreams. What did he have to offer that would challenge that? He'd known that from the first day, that first kiss. So why did her leaving hurt so much now?

He bent down and braced himself to take Tilly's weight as the door to the cottage opened.

'It's Kate!' Jemima said, unbuckling her belt and tearing towards the door.

Gideon allowed himself a quick glance up. He was in time to see Kate bending down to hug Jemima as she rushed towards her.

She's leaving, he reminded himself. She doesn't want this. He picked up the sleepy Tilly and headed towards the cottage.

Kate set Jemima back down on her feet and looked up at him. 'Is Emily able to help you?'

'Yes.' He pushed past and started to climb the stairs.

'Gideon, I—'

'Not now. I can't talk now.'

Kate glanced across at Jemima and said no more. He carried on up the stairs, which left her standing foolishly at the bottom step. She turned and forced a smile. 'Come on, Jemima, tell me about your sleepover.'

Together they went into the kitchen and started to put together a simple tea. She could hear Gideon moving about upstairs even while she kept up with Jemima's constant stream of chatter.

As the minutes ticked by Kate's tension increased. Jemima finished her tea and started to yawn. 'Tired?' she asked, stroking the top of her head.

Jemima nodded.

'Run up to Daddy. He'll help you get into bed.'

She didn't need any further urging. Their night with Emily and her brood had left them both exhausted. Kate watched her go with a heavy heart.

And still no sign of Gideon. Kate stacked the dishwasher and wiped down the kitchen table before going through to the front parlour. The grate sat empty but tonight she had no compulsion to light a fire there.

'I think Tilly's going to be ill,' Gideon said when he came back down. 'She feels a bit hot. I've given her some medicine and she's gone to sleep now.'

Kate turned away trying desperately to hide her emotions. *It wasn't her responsibility.* He would manage without her. Emily would help.

He walked across and poured himself a glass of brandy. 'Want any?'

She shook her head. Gideon replaced the stopper in the cut glass decanter and placed it back on the sideboard. He took his glass and walked over to one of the chairs, sitting down with his elbows resting on his knees.

He swirled the liquid in his glass. 'Have you found out whether you can get a ferry tomorrow?'

Kate nodded. 'There's no problem. It's a Monday. Not many people are wanting to leave the island.'

Gideon glanced up. 'No. I suppose not.'

'It's for the best,' Kate said. She stood up and walked towards the door, her arms folded in front of her chest. 'How did you imagine we were going to play this? We could hardly have a full-blown affair in front of the children. And we're both too old to go skulking about.'

He sipped his drink. 'Skulking' was such an ugly word. Didn't she realise how much he loved her? That he was hoping for so much more than an affair?

Obviously not. His eyes took in her defensive posture. She wanted to go. And he loved her enough to want to make that easy. He looked up. 'I'll miss you.'

She swallowed, then nodded. 'I'll miss you too.' Her chin raised slightly. 'I've booked myself on an early ferry. I'll try and see the girls before I go, but if I don't...'

'I'll tell them,' he said without looking up.

He heard Kate's deep intake of breath. 'Right. I'll go and finish my packing.'

Then he heard the sound of the door closing.

Kate rounded the final corner. Not taking the car had seemed such a good idea when she'd left home that morning. Saving money on the congestion charge for one thing, not losing her parking space another.

But now her hands were sore from the handles on

her heavy shopping bags and her toes scrunched from the black stilettos she'd bought on the Isle of Wight.

She put the bags down on the pavement to give her palms a break, glancing up at the green doorway a short distance away. Nearly home.

If you could call it home. It didn't feel like a home. It was just a place to sleep. A cold, empty place in a big city.

There was no comparison between that and the picture-book country cottage Gideon called home. She missed it. She missed the sounds of Jemima and Tilly playing. She missed Gideon walking through the door at the end of a long evening. She missed seeing him at breakfast, the shared laughter and having someone to talk to.

She missed him.

And she hated knowing she'd run away because she'd been too scared to stay.

Wearily, she went to pick up her shopping bags, and a shadow fell across her. She looked up swiftly.

Gideon. Here. Her exhausted mind struggled to process how that could be possible. Gideon in London? That wasn't right. He should be on the Isle of Wight. With his children.

'Hello,' he said simply.

Kate let the bags fall back on the pavement. 'What are you doing here?'

'Waiting for you.'

It was no answer at all, but at that moment it seemed quite sensible. 'Is everything all right? With Debbie?' she asked, suddenly worried that might be the reason he was here.

'Debbie's fine.'

'Oh.' Kate eyes raked his face, searching for the reason he was here.

He looked tired, the lines on his face more accentuated than she'd ever seen them. But still gorgeous. Tall, handsome and strong. Slightly aloof now, dressed in a sharp grey suit and black shirt.

Perhaps he'd had a meeting in London? Was that why he was here? Kate ran a distracted hand through her hair, conscious that she looked as if she was at the end of a long day. But he was still here. Outside her flat and waiting for her. He must want to see her.

Gideon changed his grip on the handle of his briefcase. 'Debbie asked me to bring you something.'

Her heart, which had started to soar, plummeted.

'She said it would be important to you.'

Kate frowned, uncertain about why Debbie would ask Gideon to bring it. She'd spoken to her last night and she hadn't mentioned anything. 'I don't understand what—'

'She found it last night among Babs's papers.'

'Oh. I see.' She bent to pick up her bags. Actually, she still didn't understand. Why did that mean Gideon was in London? 'You'd better come in, then.'

His hand came out to stop her. Silently he took the shopping from her and started down the street towards her front door.

Kate took a moment before following him. She had to run a bit to catch up with him. 'I'm on the first floor.'

Three and a half weeks since she'd seen him but he'd been in her mind all that time. *Had he thought about her at all?*

They walked into the communal hall and up the stairs to her flat.

Dear God. She couldn't do this. She wanted to reach out and touch him. She wanted to beg him to love her.

'How are the girls?' she asked, stepping into the narrow hallway. 'Are they in London with you?'

Gideon followed her into the tiny kitchenette and placed the bags on the worktop, his briefcase on the floor.

He glanced down at his Rolex. 'By now they'll be having tea at Debbie's. It's gone six.'

Kate took off her coat and hung it in the hall cupboard.

His eyes followed her. 'Debbie took them to Nursery and school this morning.'

'Oh,' Kate said inanely, coming back to stand in the kitchen. She didn't understand this at all. *Why* was he in London?

She fiddled about unloading the bags, conscious of the tinned soup, the bottled sauces and the ready-to-heat meals.

'But they're fine.' He paused. 'Missing you...but fine.'

Kate looked up. His hands were thrust deep in his trouser pockets.

'We're all missing you,' he said, and his words seemed to throb through her body as though they were an electric current. His blue eyes were fixed on hers. They never wavered.

Her hands hovered over the bag and then they dropped to her sides. 'Why are you in London? Did you have a meeting or something?'

'I had a meeting in Southampton but...Debbie changed my plans.'

Kate frowned.

'So I got on the train and came up here.' He paused, then asked quietly. 'Why didn't you tell me, Kate?'

Her eyes flew to his face. 'A-about?'

'That you can't have children?'

His words hung in the air between them. Kate almost stepped backwards with the impact of them.

'Debbie told you?' she whispered. *She couldn't believe that.* Why would Debbie have done that?

'She thought I knew. She thought you'd have told me.' He spoke quietly. 'You should have told me, Kate.'

Kate struggled to hold back the tears. 'I know. I'm sorry.' She turned and went to sit on the cream sofa. 'I don't tell anyone. Ever. I won't have people feeling sorry for me. Debbie shouldn't have said anything.'

She was aware that he'd turned away. He went to the breakfast bar and picked up his briefcase.

'She found this.' His fingers flicked the lock open and he pulled out a battered scrapbook. 'It was amongst Babs's things.'

He came back to the sofa and handed it to her, his eyes watching her face.

Kate opened the first cover. Inside there was a small photograph, bent across the corner. Kate didn't need to read the inscription written underneath in Babs's familiar looped writing. She remembered the day that it had been taken. What surprised her was why Babs had it.

The photograph had been taken at the last children's home she'd stayed at. Months before she'd been sent to the Isle of Wight.

She'd been stood on the grey steps outside the dark blue painted door and told to smile. She hadn't, of course. Her angry little face stared straight at the camera. Underneath Aunt Babs had written a simple *My Katie* and the date.

Kate glanced up at Gideon; his eyes were still watching her. Gauging her reaction, it seemed. She turned the page and saw more photographs. There was one of her first Christmas on the Isle of Wight. Her fringe had been cut straight by then and she looked almost happy.

Photo after photo. The card she'd made at school on Mother's Day and had given to Aunt Babs. Her flute grade certificates all carefully stuck in. All her school reports. As she reached the end Gideon handed her a second volume.

'I can't believe she did this,' she said, her eyes filling up with tears. It was a complete record of her life.

'She loved you.'

The words caressed her. *Loved. She'd been loved.*

'She also wrote you a letter.' Gideon passed across the white envelope he'd been holding. 'It was in the front of one of the scrapbooks.'

Aunt Babs had addressed it to 'Kate'. Just her name. Her fingers shook as she opened it. Inside was a single sheet of spaced writing. She glanced up at Gideon and then back to the paper.

Darling Kate, I couldn't have loved you more if you'd been born to me.

Kate could almost hear her voice saying the words—she'd said them many times over the years— but reading them gave them a stronger impact.

Not a child of my body, but a child of my heart. Chosen to be part of my family. My daughter in every way that matters.

It was my privilege to share your life. You were born with such talent and I loved giving you the opportunity to use it. I have loved seeing you grow from a young girl to the beautiful woman you are now. I am so proud of you.

My Kate.

Life brings all kinds of disappointments. You have already had more than your fair share, I know. But being a mother is not an accident of birth, Kate. It comes from a decision to love, to care and to nurture. It takes courage, and that you have in abundance.

Remember this: your mother gave you life but I was there to nurture it. She saw your first smile but I was there to calm your fears and share your triumphs.

God bless, my Kate. Choose well.

Kate carefully folded the paper along the creases already there, tears welling up and trickling down her face.

Gideon sat beside her, his arms coming to hold her against the warm protection of his body. 'Kate.' He breathed her name into her hair as his arms held her close. 'Don't. I can't bear to see you cry.'

His hand reached out to brush the last remaining tears from her face. And then he groaned and pulled her in close. Kate went unresisting, her head coming to rest on his chest.

'Do you know what she wrote?' Kate asked slowly.

He shook his head. 'I haven't read your letter, if that's what you mean. Debbie said it was important and...I brought it to you. I love you, Kate.'

His words were so quiet she wasn't sure she'd heard them. She looked up, her eyes fearful and questioning. His gaze met hers.

Gideon's mouth twisted. 'I love you,' he repeated. 'I know you don't want to hear it, that you've got a life to lead here, but...'

And then she knew what Aunt Babs had been trying to tell her—that all men weren't like Richard. That the ability to have a baby shouldn't define her life. That there were children like her, children who needed love as she had done. *Children like Jemima and Tilly.*

'When I was twenty-two,' she began quietly, 'I was rushed to the hospital with stomach pains. I had a ruptured appendix, which caused some damage to one of my fallopian tubes.'

Gideon reached for her hand and held it. 'They discovered then that my ovaries hadn't developed properly.'

'Why didn't you tell me before?' he asked quietly.

'B-because...' Kate turned her face away. 'Richard left me because he wanted children. Because I'm not enough on my own.'

He frowned. 'And you thought I wouldn't want you if you told me?'

She nodded miserably.

His arms immediately came round her, his strength completely enfolding her, protecting her. Giving her hope.

'Was that why you left?'

Kate tried to answer but her voice wouldn't work.

Her unshed tears were burning the back of her throat like acid.

His fingers moved to stroke her hair. 'Kate, when Laura died—' he began, and then stopped speaking, his mind searching for the words. He started again. 'Laura changed after Jemima was born. It was like a blanket had been put over her personality and, in a sense, I lost her then.'

Kate stayed still, listening intently to every word he was saying. His fingers moved softly against her hair.

'Then Laura fell pregnant a second time. It wasn't planned, at least not by me. Sometimes I wondered… Anyway, the midwife was quite encouraging. Laura would be monitored. She'd be given medication quickly if she needed it.'

Gideon shifted in his seat. Kate looked up. His eyes showed a fierce kind of pain.

'Don't tell me. I don't need to know.'

He took her face between his hands. 'Yes, you do, Kate. I love my girls, God help me. But I never want to experience anything like that again.'

Kate nodded, but she didn't really understand what he was trying to tell her.

'I told myself I didn't want another relationship.' His smile twisted. 'Then you came back to the island. And you weren't what I was expecting.' His thumb moved across her cheek. 'I knew you were beautiful…and clever. But I didn't know you would break through every barrier I'd erected round me.'

Kate didn't dare breathe. It was as if sunshine had broken through dark clouds and was flooding her world with light.

'I think I fell in love with you at Babs's funeral. I

promised myself, after we kissed, that I'd keep away from you. You were dangerous and I knew it.'

Happiness was unfurling inside her like the beginnings of a rosebud taking shape.

'And young. No children and you were bound to want them. You were absolutely not what I wanted.'

He reached out and stroked the side of her face. 'Then you moved into my home and I knew that I was completely lost. I spent hours agonising over whether I could go through the whole ordeal again.

'And then I reasoned that you wouldn't want what I could offer anyway. A widower with two children— how attractive was that going to be to a career-minded television journalist? I might as well take whatever you could give me.

'I knew you'd leave me. But I didn't know how much that would hurt. It's been three weeks of hell without you.'

'You love me?' Kate asked, her brown eyes shimmering with tears.

Gideon moved so he could see into her face more clearly. 'Didn't you know?'

She shook her head. 'You never said. When I saw you with little Katie, at the hospital…I knew I had to go.'

'Why?' he asked, his forehead furrowed.

'Because I'd always be second best,' she said simply. 'I was playing at keeping house, being part of your life. You'd shared such incredible moments with Laura and I knew I couldn't compete.'

His eyes softened as though he understood all she was trying to tell him but couldn't find the words. And she knew the moment he decided to kiss her.

Gideon's eyes flicked to her lips and back to her

eyes. Kate moved towards him, her arms snaking up round his neck and her fingers burying themselves in his thick hair.

At last he pulled away and settled her back in the curve of his arm. 'I love you, Kate. With or without children. I want you. Just you—because I'm not happy without you.'

Kate let her head rest on his chest. 'I love you too. I think I've always loved you but I was too scared to tell you.'

He kissed the top of her head. 'How are we going to manage this?' he asked, holding her close. 'It'll take a bit of sorting, but I can get Anton to take on the management of the Quay Inn. I'll pull out of my project on the mainland, but I've still got to find somewhere to live that'll work for Jemima and Tilly.'

'Leave the island?' Kate turned in his arms. 'But you love it there. And the restaurant…'

His face softened as he looked down at her. 'I love you more.'

More! It was as if she'd been offered the world. He'd leave everything he loved for her. He'd uproot his children and settle them in a strange city. For her.

'No.'

His face shadowed. 'No?'

She shook her head. 'I don't want you to do that. I'll come to the island. If you want me.'

'I can't let you give up the career you've been working so hard for.'

Kate smiled up at him. 'It's no different for you. Is it?'

Her smile broadened as he couldn't answer. 'I can write my column from anywhere.' She threaded her hand into his. 'Let me come home. You're all I've ever wanted. You—and your girls.'

Gideon leant over and kissed her gently on the lips. 'On one condition.'

'What's that?'

'Marry me?' he asked softly, his blue eyes gazing into her brown ones. 'Marry me. I need to know you're never going to disappear out of my life again.'

Kate didn't need to think. She wrapped her arms tightly round him. 'Yes, please.'

She was finally coming home, to a family of her own.